ELLE BEAUMONT

A HORDE OF DEAD POETS

DEATH'S MAIDEN

ELLE BEAUMONT

PERCY'S HEART PRESS

Percy's Heart Press www.percysheartpress.com

Book Layout

Edited by Carla Lewis, Jess Moore

Cover Art and Design © 2024 Adina Chiles

Interior Formatting by Book Savvy Services

Credit to: Kipling, Rudyard. "The Undertaker's Horse", *Departmental Ditties and Other Verses*, 1886

To those who taught me how to live fully and those who taught me how to say goodbye, to the beauty in beginnings and the grace in letting go.

Answer, sombre beast and dreary,
Where is Brown, the young, the cheery,
Smith, the pride of all his friends and half the
    Force?
You were at that last dread dak
We must cover at a walk,
Bring them back to me, O Undertaker's
    Horse!

With your mane unhogged and flowing,
And your curious way of going,
And that businesslike black crimping of your
    tail,
E'en with Beauty on your back, Sir,
Pacing as a lady's hack, Sir,
What wonder when I meet you I turn pale?

Rudyard Kipling
"The Undertaker's Horse"

Contents

Prologue

The gods slumbered.

Five hundred and thirty years ago had been the last time their gods had awakened, walked among their land, and reduced the nearby villages to cinders. So, the people of Svetl never prayed for mercy, because they already knew their gods were vengeful.

Golden light flickered against the walls of the Great Lodge as hundreds of tallow candles lined the altar. Long, wooden benches remained empty, but they wouldn't for long, not when the villagers of Svetl would spill in, gathering to talk of their recent victories, be it boasting of their fishing, or conquering a neighboring foe.

Svetl was in a time of peace with their neighbors, but as with most things in life, it came in waves.

Eirunn had been born in a time when even her parents hadn't seen battle, yet warriors still trained. But at the age of twelve, she knew she didn't want to hold a shield or sword, battling her brothers and sisters. What Eirunn wanted was to help and to heal. Like Bodin.

She swallowed and walked up the stairs to the platform. Six carvings of their gods and goddesses stood in a *v* formation: Hakan the Father and Supreme one; Gyda the Mother; Sassa the Beauty; Roska the Fierce; Bodin the Caretaker; and Njal the Warrior.

And carved on the platform was a lantern and a shroud of darkness, symbolizing Life and Death. Two entities not of the godly world, but of the living realm. Set apart from the heavens yet still watched.

Eirunn reached out and brushed her fingers along the engraved wood. Bodin's kind and handsome face smiled at his people. She tried to imagine the god, who sought to nurture flora and fauna, so angered that he'd side with destroying them all.

Her skin prickled at the back of her neck, and she spun on her heel, feeling as though someone or something was watching her. "Tyr, if that's you, it isn't funny." He was always trying to scare her, but when he didn't answer and she didn't see his shadow, her heart inched up her throat.

You have nothing to fear, maiden. A deep voice snaked throughout the lodge. Eirunn caught sight of a shadow crawling up the exposed beams, seeming to purposefully remain away from the skylight.

"What are you?" Her voice shook as she backed into the carvings. *No. She hadn't woken one of the gods, had she?* Fearful, she peered around, but nothing else was out of sorts. The candles scarcely flickered, even with the shadow darting around.

The being formed before her, and Eirunn's eyes couldn't focus on the apparition for too long. It was like trying to make a figure out in the early morning light. Her eyes played tricks on her, and it appeared to jerk, or maybe the shadows wavered like a banner in the wind, but when she refocused, the creature was as still as could be.

What am I? The voice rumbled and swiveled around her. *You could ask who I am, but you ask* what? It hummed. *I am the quiet that follows the last beat of a heart. The shadow that waits at the edge of every light. I am the inevitable pause to your fleeting song.*

Eirunn gasped and quickly retreated down the steps toward the long benches. She nearly fell as she bumped into one, but her eyes remained on the undulating figure. "You are...Death." She swallowed roughly and glanced toward the altar.

I am. And I'm here to claim you as my own.

"Am I dead?" Her voice quaked, and she lifted a hand to her throat.

Death laughed coldly. *No, child. I need a maiden, one who can walk between the worlds with me and reap the ripe souls.*

Tears pricked Eirunn's eyes. She was a child of spring, one who cherished life above all else. How could she be a servant of Death? "Why me? Why not someone else?"

The season has passed for my prior reaper, and with no daughter to claim, I have no choice but to search for another. The line of maidens must carry on. The shadows surrounding Death swirled, collecting themselves until a nearly solid figure stood before her. *Be at peace, young one. Death eases the struggle and weight that life brings. It is a noble thing, to die.*

To the villagers, it was an honor to die in battle, while a youth's passing was a bad omen. Eirunn had witnessed Death. Her mother died in childbirth with her little brother, who scarcely lived to see his second month.

"You took my mother away, and my little brother," she said in a rasp.

It was their time, and because I have touched one close to you, it is why I am here. Your soul has been caressed by my presence, marked for me to claim as my own.

"Do I have a choice?" She gritted her teeth, blinking away tears.

No.

Eirunn flopped onto a nearby bench and glanced up at the skylights. In one of the windows, she saw the full moon. She prayed that Bodin would take care of her, and if children were in her future, them too. And she sent up a prayer to Gyda the Mother, for that matter.

"Do you have a name other than Death?"

The apparition hummed in thought, then chuckled. *Some call me Hadeon.*

Fitting, she thought. His moniker meant destroyer.

Although you are my servant, I will allow you a request. Choose how I will appear to you and your family.

Eirunn gawked at the shadows. What did she care, as if he'd be any less of a threat in any form? "A horse as black as night, and a mane that pours down like an ebony waterfall." The moment the words left her mouth the shadows before her turned to smoke, then solidified once more. Before her stood the most impressive horse she'd ever seen.

A stallion with a proud Roman nose and bottomless brown eyes.

He was lovely.

He was *Death*.

"Will anyone else see you?" she whispered and stood. She stepped forward, afraid to touch, but too curious to abstain.

Her hand met a velveteen muzzle, but instead of warmth, there was only coldness.

Only when I want them to. He snorted. *Find me in the barn outside your dwelling and you will begin your lessons.*

The doors to the Great Lodge swung open and the boisterous laughter of her father and the jarl filled the space. Eirunn's eyes widened, panicked that she'd need to explain why she'd brought a horse into the lodge, but when she turned around, there was no one.

Come find me, Hadeon's voice echoed in her mind and when her eyes met her father's his graying brows rose in question.

"What are you doing in here by yourself?" Her father strode forward, flanked by the jarl and another warrior.

Eirunn could lie and say she was just speaking to Bodin, as she had planned to, but for some reason the truth itched the tip of her tongue. "I was talking to Death."

Neither her father nor the men by his side laughed, and she wondered what they knew, if they knew of the maidens before her.

"You spoke to Death?" her father whispered. "Don't jest, dear heart." He closed the space between them and placed his calloused hand on her shoulder. "Why are you really here?"

"I'm not jesting." She glanced up at him. "He said I am his maiden."

The jarl exchanged a glance with the man by his side, then edged forward to her. "Tell no one of what you saw and heard today. Do you understand? Dying is part of our cycle, but if someone knows a maiden is lurking about, they'll come for you in droves. Just as they did Katla."

Eirunn blanched. Katla—the cousin to the jarl—sweet Katla, who was always smiling...She was a maiden?

She had died two months ago, slaughtered in the woods like a common boar. No one knew why, nor who had done it.

With a nod, she turned on her heel to glance back at the gods. All she had wanted to do was pray to them and instead Death had come for her.

One

The moon shone high above the trees, filtering through the bare limbs and streaming into the living room. Inessa would never forget that night because it was the first time she'd seen *him* for what he was.

Death.

Father paced in front of the hearth. His elk-skin boots scuffed the rough pine floor as he shook his head. "Not her. Not her," he muttered, then quickly walked to a cot where Mother lay.

She had been sick with fever for over a week now and even at twelve, Inessa knew it didn't bode well, especially in the deep winter of Svetl.

"Eirunn isn't supposed to die. She can't!" Father's voice took on an accusatory note.

"Father," she whispered, ignoring the knitting of emotions in her chest. "Is she..." Reluctantly, Inessa stepped forward and crouched next to the cot. Several fur blankets covered her mother's still form. She frowned and took up her frail hand.

It was cold, despite being under the heavy furs, next to the blazing hearth.

"Inessa," her mother gasped. "You must look Death in the eyes and..."

At first, Inessa didn't think her mother would finish, and even more worrisome was the rattling breath she drew in. But her mother was healthy, or at least had been before Death kissed her.

"You must accept...Death." She sucked in air, and her head fell onto the pillow once again. "You belong to him as much as he belongs to you."

These words made no sense to Inessa. Her mother was uttering nonsense, but when she looked at her father, he simply stared into the leaping flames, frowning. Delirium must have taken her already, and that realization formed a gaping hole inside of Inessa's chest.

"Father," she said, voice breaking.

"You are the undertaker's daughter," he murmured. "And Death's maiden."

"I don't understand!" Lightning struck and Inessa leaped away from her mother's sickbed and clutched at her chest. It was as if she could feel her heart shattering.

The barn doors flapped violently outside, drumming a beat she knew well during windstorms. But a new rhythm took place, one that sounded so much like the pounding of skin drums.

She stared down at her mother, and despite the warmth of the small cottage, Inessa watched silvery vapors leave her mother's mouth. She squinted, wondering if her eyes deceived her. What threads were those? "Mother?" Inessa rushed forward, kneeling next to her. She gripped her mother's bicep, squeezing lightly. "Mother?" Panic lanced through her chest, and she shook her mother by the shoulders. "No! No! Come back to me!"

Inessa threw herself onto the cot, hoping to hear the rhythmic *thud-thud*. But there was nothing—no rise and fall of her mother's chest, no beating of her heart.

"Inessa," her father called softly. His arms encircled her, and he pulled her away. "He'll be coming for you."

Who? She wanted to scream, but she couldn't find her voice beyond the sobs.

A pounding against the cottage wall gave both her and her father a start. Inessa dragged her blurry vision to the window, and she wished she hadn't.

From outside, yellow glowing eyes watched them. Eyes that she should've known, yet they were so vastly different from their normal deep brown.

Hadeon.

Her mother's horse. Black as night, with a crimped mane and tail so thick it took Inessa hours to comb and braid it. His rounded nose gave him a stately appearance, but the town loathed him for what he represented whenever her father trotted by with the wagon in tow.

Death.

Hadeon pulled the carriage as Father collected the departed from their homes. He transported them to their graveyards, and all that watched as he trotted by trembled with the fear they might be next.

But Hadeon had let her ride him to the river and spent so many hours running freely through the overgrown meadows. How many times had she braided his forelock?

Another flash of lightning illuminated the equine's face. He shook his thick mane out, and Inessa knew she wasn't imagining it when she felt his eyes peer into the depths of her soul, claiming her.

Bound to serve.

Bound to Death.

"Inessa, look at me. You cannot run from him, my girl." Her father rasped and wrapped an arm around her, holding her close to his chest. "He will find you and there is no avoiding his claiming." Sorrow pooled in his gaze.

"I don't want to accept him, and I don't want to accept her Death! Sh-she's gone!" Inessa hiccuped as she sobbed. "I want her back!" And despite her sadness, a growing fury blossomed in her. Her father had known, and he'd kept this from her. "You knew though. You knew she would die?" Inessa yanked herself away from him, feeling the deepest of betrayals. Why would he keep this from her? She wanted to vomit. "Why?" she wailed and rubbed her eyes furiously.

"Your mother didn't want you to know. She wanted you to live as normal a life as possible." He approached her slowly, as if she were a feral beast on the verge of fleeing, and maybe she was. However, he stopped himself and turned back to his wife—her mother—and choked on a sob. "Until we meet again." He pulled the fur up over her and shot an accusatory glance toward the window. Hadeon was still pounding away.

"Make him stop."

"I wish I could, my girl." Her father led her out of the bedroom and into their humble dining quarter. The heart roared with a blazing fire, casting shadows along the wooden walls. "Sit."

She complied, though everything in her screamed to run back to her mother's side. But she was gone. Maybe if she prayed to Hakan, the Supreme One, he'd wake and breathe life into her once again. But the gods were never merciful, and so what was the point? Even Bodin, the great caretaker, wouldn't offer his assistance. At least, not that she had ever seen.

"Your mother was chosen as a maiden when she was your age. And...she didn't want you to have to carry this burden." He rubbed his eyes and crossed the room to lean against the fire mantle. "She didn't want to have children because she knew it would mean Hadeon could claim them."

Precisely what she wanted to hear at the moment—that her mother wished she'd never been born. Clenching her fists, she placed them on the table, listening but unwilling to speak.

"Except I came into the picture and your mother thought that maybe she could find someone else to take her place, so that she could spare her children." He cleared his throat. "Inessa, your mother loved you more than life itself. Remember how much she loved life, how much she loved living."

Inessa, come to me. A gravelly voice rolled around in her head. She didn't have to guess; she simply knew it was Hadeon.

Two

SIXTEEN YEARS LATER

Little Vanja Skorsen sat on a log in front of Inessa, wriggling. "I can't finish your braids if you don't sit still," she said with laughter. The blond child stilled for a moment, until Inessa began tightly braiding her hair again. It was difficult to see with the fading sunlight. Soon, the moon and stars would shine brightly. "Well, Vanja, don't come to me to fix your braids when they fall out in two nights time." She clucked her tongue and chuckled when the girl grew as still as a stump.

When she finished, Vanja hopped up and hugged her tightly. "I'll find someone else then." She wrinkled her nose, then bounded off to run with her friends around the blazing bonfire.

Being that it was the dead of winter, it was frigid, but that was to be expected in Svetl. The nights were long, days short, and both were brisk enough to freeze a person in place.

Although, Inessa always ran colder than the average person. The air didn't sting her as much as it might her father or friend, Einar.

Svetl was a smaller village in the forest alongside Ljus Lake. Villagers fished all year long, even in the months when the lake was frozen solid and they had to cut holes to lower a hook with bait on a rope into the depths.

The winters were harsh, but the villagers were accustomed to it. Every home boasted a massive hearth, and furs were plentiful now that a new truce with the neighboring village of Runestadt had formed.

That had happened only last year, and had Jarl Vilmar not stepped in, pleading for a resolution, there would have been many lives lost.

Sometimes Inessa wished she had her mother's ability to remain lighthearted amid bleakness. Laughing without a care, inspiring everyone around her to live, despite being a maid of Death. Inessa couldn't forgive as readily, couldn't forget serious transgressions the way her mother could. Not when those of Runestadt had purposely hunted their food and raided their store houses.

Even though they didn't need any of it.

Try as she might, Inessa could never be the woman her mother was. At twenty-eight years old, her mother had already wed, had a child and a whole life. Inessa had...complications.

It had been sixteen years since her mother passed. Sixteen years since she'd been claimed as Death's maiden, and she had tried to live as normally as she could.

In her teenhood and early twenties, she had trained to become a fierce battle maiden—a rarity in their land—and had climbed the rankings with tenacity. Except, in a time where there were no battles, no wars, what good was a battle maiden?

It only led to times of indulgence for her. Nothing more than a tumble here or there with a few of the villagers.

Einar Jorgensen, her childhood friend, and for a time, fancy, made his way toward her and extended his calloused hand. He grinned and offered a wink. "Come on, Inessa, join the revelry." She grabbed his hand, and with one firm tug, she collided with his chest. He smelled of pine trees and sweet ale. His dark blue eyes twinkled with mischief. She had half a mind to yank on his braided auburn hair.

Sometimes, she wished that things had worked between them. His playfulness always brought a smile to her face, but it wasn't enough. She didn't love him and a part of her wondered if love would ever be possible for her. It had been for her mother.

"Are you certain I won't cast a shadow over the festivities?"

Einar snorted and stepped away, but he kept his arm around her so that she had no choice but to remain tucked against his side. "The most absurd thing I've ever heard. And I've heard plenty."

"I am the equivalent to a wet woolen blanket on a cold winter's night," she said in a theatrical tone, laughing at the end.

Einar shot her a contemplative look. "No. You're more like a late autumn morning. Crisp, with a hint of warmth and the comfort of a roaring fire."

His words took her by surprise. Inessa's mouth fell open and she laughed a moment later. "Einar, that was the sweetest thing you've ever said to me apart from calling me a brutish fighter."

She may not have been a wet woolen blanket, but it hadn't been easy growing up the undertaker's daughter either. Death was part of their life and falling in battle was honorable, but dying in one's sleep? Succumbing to illness? Snatching a babe from their mother, or worse, stealing the breath from both mother and babe? It wasn't honorable, it wasn't sought after, and it was unfair.

And since there were no battles, most Deaths occurred naturally, and the idea of honorable Deaths faded away. The elders, like Einar's mother, Val, believed in being touched by the gods and daemons. She loathed Inessa, believed her to be touched by Death and she wasn't wrong.

Einar led her toward the bonfire, which blazed next to one of the two-story wooden homes. The fire stretched toward the sky, climbing the stacked wood which easily reached the height of three tall men. Halved logs formed makeshift seats a distance away, and those who were not dancing or standing were seated, watching as the flames lapped at the darkening heavens.

Here, among the people, she almost felt as though she could blend in and simply be one of them. But the truth of her identity kept her from forming close bonds, not because she didn't love them, for she did greatly. It caused her great pain whenever she stole a last breath from one of them.

"Oh, don't look now. My mother is warding you off, I think."

Inessa had already seen as his mother made a sign of protection with her fingers, warding off malicious spirits with her fore and middle finger splayed apart.

Sometimes, Inessa wondered if one of the gods had touched Einar's mother. Since her suspicions of Inessa's ties with Death were so spot on, she wondered if the old woman could see Hadeon.

She looked away, shaking her head. "It didn't work when

I was twelve and it won't work now." Val Jorgensen was the most superstitious woman in the village. She thought Inessa was a daemon that walked the land, but a daemon paled in comparison to what Inessa could do. Did that make her worse? Likely.

Drums clattered behind her as they were rolled out, and boisterous laughter filled the area as the ale flowed. The mouthwatering aroma of smoked boar tickled her nose, reminding her she hadn't eaten yet.

"Go find a woman to lay with tonight and I'm going to stuff myself until I'm as round as Grigor." She winked and pulled away from him, not needing his charity, although it was greatly appreciated. "Go, you lovable oaf."

Vanja ran up to her, grabbing her by the waist. "Dance with us, Nes!" She tugged gently.

Inessa glanced around, seeing a gathering of most of Svetl's children ranging in age from six all the way to sixteen. The older ones oversaw tending to the younger, and in the firelight, Inessa spotted hints of annoyance on a few of the older children's faces. Their tones too harsh, their mouth in a scowl.

She chuckled and followed Vanja, allowing herself to enjoy the small bit of revelry, for the tide would change soon, she had no doubt.

She was Death's Maiden, after all.

Three

Inessa's breath billowed in visible clouds. It was the sort of cold that made one's bones ache to the marrow. Just three nights ago she had been dancing around a fire with children, and now, beneath the silver light of the moon, she had to reap.

She grimaced and straightened, stretching her back, as Hadeon led the way through the heavily trodden path in the woods. When Inessa rode him, it brought memories flooding back to her of braiding his mane. When she was a girl, she'd wondered why Hadeon had let her. He'd told her it was to strengthen their bond—servant and master. Now, she saw it for what it had been, trickery. But it was an old offense that she shrugged off now.

When they'd been together, her mother had always watched them with a curious gleam in her eye. Inessa didn't know it then, of course, but that gleam was the knowledge that one day her daughter would carry her same burden of reaping.

Lit by the moon, they traveled through the dense pine forest, away from Svetl.

"Where are we heading tonight?" she asked quietly. Though it wasn't necessary to whisper, the woods were so quiet it would sound like she was yelling if she hadn't.

"Skaldfjord."

A village beyond Runestadt even. It would take most of the night to travel there and she wouldn't return home until close to midday on the morrow. By now, most of Svetl would be asleep and those who weren't, and happened to be on the road, wouldn't see Inessa or Hadeon. She had learned early on that he could glamour not only himself, but her as well when it came time to reap.

Throughout the journey, the moon shifted, forcing Inessa to call upon her preternatural eyesight. A gift, along with an assortment of others, from Hadeon. She could see in dim light, not quite as well as if it were day, but along the lines of what she assumed a wolf might see at night.

The road widened, then gave way to an open sky. Immediately, Inessa noticed that the homes were built in the old way. The roof lines were triangular shaped and came to the ground. Sod covered the roofs, half hidden by a coating of snow. The closest home had a wisp of smoke exiting a small window at the top, no doubt from a struggling fire.

She had little doubt that every home had a hearth roaring, or sputtering, as the villagers slept heavily.

Someone here would not awaken to another sunrise.

Inessa chewed the inside of her cheek and sighed. Gone were the conflicting emotions of reaping. This was who she was, what she had been born to do. However, she'd be lying if she said she'd grown callous to the loss of life, because Inessa did have that part of her mother inside of her.

"Every life is precious, Inessa. Even those who have wronged us," her mother used to say.

A hard truth to swallow as a girl. Easy enough to say a life wasn't valuable when one wasn't facing a trembling babe, or a wheezing old man...

Inessa hopped down, hesitating near Hadeon's flank. She scanned the village, waiting for it—the pulse of the dying soul.

A moment passed, then two before a steady thrumming called to her. Like the beating of a blackbird's wings, one spirit fluttered and pulsed, drawing her across the grounds.

Inessa opened the wooden door to a stranger's home and stepped inside. Unlike most of the homes in Svetl, there were no rooms in this structure, just a single open space. To her left, the family gathered with their pallets; the mother huddled near her adolescent son. Even from here, Inessa could hear the boy's rattling breath.

An aura, as if moonlight had spilled, glowed distinctly around his form. His soul beckoned, like a lantern in a blizzard.

She glanced aside, seeing their well-loved table, covered in stains and markings. Full of memories and love.

Inessa swallowed roughly, turned away from the table, and crept toward the sleeping boy.

You are taking far too long.

He could bite her.

Shaking her head, she gently touched the boy's damp brow. The halo of light around him burned brighter, as if her very presence alerted his soul—it was time.

"May the Great Stallion guide you to the Hall," Inessa murmured as she caressed his youthful cheek, then closed her eyes.

Harvesting a soul had been tricky the first time or two. The essence of a soul was similar to a spider's silk, twisting and snaking as she coaxed it from its host. Then, as the last strand tugged free of the person, the cord straightened and disappeared, vanishing into the afterlife. Not every soul was cooperative, and some forced her to yank their strands free. This boy, he was more than ready. His skin was wan, and his lips had developed a blue tint. Inessa assumed if he opened his eyes they'd have a dull appearance. Poor boy. She could feel his surrender as his soul almost overwhelmed her, eagerly fleeing from its prolonged existence on this plane, and then he exhaled, making the final pass.

The tension that always seemed to build during the harvesting released as soon as the deed was done.

Inessa loosed a breath, then crept out of the home as quietly as she had came. When she mounted Hadeon, a great sob tore through the air.

It is done.

Inessa huffed and cast her eyes toward the thick brush. She could've sworn something had moved there. A flash of white fur. A deer maybe? A wolf wasn't that tall...it could be a bear. Her skin prickled. It was as if someone watched her, but that was impossible—no one could see her.

"Do you feel that?" she whispered, finding herself unable to explain the *feeling*.

Hadeon's flank twitched in rapid succession. Despite being Death, he still acted quite like a horse, and by that twitch, she knew he grew nervous. If he wanted to, he could dissipate and leave her stranded, but there was a sliver of loyalty between them after all the years.

I don't know what it is, Hadeon said, agitation clear in his tone.

His not knowing didn't inspire comfort in her. Again, her skin prickled, the hair rising at the back of her neck, and she glanced around.

A deer wouldn't make her feel as though she were being hunted.

Inessa swept her gaze along the tree line.

Nothing.

She sighed and blinked as snow started to fall, catching in her lashes. "I don't want to be caught in a storm, or by a pack of wolves, let's go." Preferably before the snow grew too deep, and they had half a day's travel yet.

INESSA HAD TAKEN A BRIEF NAP WHEN SHE returned home, but there was much to be done. Especially with the fresh blanket of snow covering the ground.

The late afternoon sun was weak and held little warmth as it shone in the orange and purple tinted sky. Despite a cool wind winding through the trees, her hands were warm and even sweating as she gripped her axe and split a log in two. The pieces fell to the ground, joining the other halves at the base of the stump.

Inessa paused after a while, wiped the fine sheen of perspiration from her brow, and set the axe down. One glance at the graying sky and gathering heavy dark clouds was all she needed to see to prepare for another bout of snow. Last night the snow had only accumulated to her calf. Maybe they'd be lucky and receive less this night. She worried about her father. She hadn't seen him since arriving home, and she wondered where he had gone too. Since there was no body to prepare for a burial, he should have been here.

The sound of boots crunching against the snow startled Inessa, and she whirled around to face her father. Exhaustion lined his features.

"Where have you been?" She cocked her head.

"I should be asking you the same thing," her father retorted with a snort. "I didn't sleep a wink last night. Not with the wind howling, not with you gone. You should get some rest." He lifted two woolen bags. "I grabbed some vegetables from Lars."

Inessa nodded. A night's full rest sounded pleasant, or even a day's worth of sleep. When she was young, Hadeon kept her to Svetl and so the reapings were not frequent. Slowly, he'd pushed her to Runestadt, to Skaldfjord, and farther. She had been gone days before. And she'd seen the toll it had taken on her father. The same dark circles beneath his eyes, the hollowness of his spirit .

In her youth, after her mother passed, she had tried to deny Hadeon, tried to ignore the compulsion to mount the horse and ride toward Death's victim. However with every attempt at resistance, the more Hadeon compelled her, only relenting when she obeyed.

The last time she had ignored him, he made her so ill she couldn't rise from her bed the next day.

"Gone that long just for vegetables?" Inessa pressed her lips together and narrowed her eyes. "I don't believe that."

Her father chuckled. "All right. I went ice fishing too, maybe dipped into some of Lars's honey mead."

Inessa stepped closer to him and took in a breath. "I can smell it on you." She gave a mock look of judgment and gripped the handle of the axe again. "At least someone has been gathering wood before the next storm rolls in."

He grunted and scratched his neck. Father wanted to say

something—he always did. It seemed as if he wanted to apologize to her, but what was there to apologize for? They all had parts to play. He the undertaker, she the reaper—Death's tool.

"Before you come in, tend to your mare. She was temperamental this morning. Then, for the love of Gyda, get some sleep."

She laughed. "All right. Just a few more logs." She swung the axe over her shoulder and watched as her father entered their home, then went back to chopping wood.

Once she was done, she piled the wood closer to the house, then wound her way around the tall oak at the side of her yard and toward the rickety paddock. Her mare, Tasha, whirled her head in annoyance, then nickered to her softly.

The dark bay mare trotted up to the fence, nostrils flaring as she bent her head to sniff Inessa's hand. She licked her sweaty palm and tossed her head, her thick forelock shifting to reveal her white star.

"Tomorrow we will go for a ride. Let me rest tonight, and tomorrow is ours."

As long as Hadeon stayed at bay.

Four

The golden light of a new morning spilled into the barn. Tasha pawed at the straw impatiently as she waited in her stall. Apparently, Inessa was taking too long tacking her up. She laughed and scanned the empty stall next to her horse.

Sometimes Hadeon would take up residence inside the barn, but he didn't need warmth, nor did he need sustenance to live. He wasn't a true horse. He was an ethereal being, who could vanish and appear at any time he wished. Death wasn't bound to a mortal plane and therefore didn't play by its rules.

Inessa hoisted the saddle into her arms and carried it into her mare's stall. "Settle down, we're going." She quickly finished tacking Tasha up, then led her outside and mounted her.

Tasha jigged in place, then trotted through the open paddock gate and onto the frozen path.

Without Hadeon's presence looming over her, Inessa's shoulders relaxed and her chest didn't feel nearly as tight.

Although she'd grown used to performing her tasks, it didn't make reaping any easier.

Moments like these, when the reapings attempted to surface in the stillness of her thoughts, Inessa took to singing. It seemed the only thing to block out the memories. Her voice filled the woods as she rode, soft and low. It was the same lullaby her mother would sing while they prepared supper, low and gentle, soothing even.

Tasha rounded the bend of the woods, and her hooves struck the dirt road that led to the main part of the village. Log homes sat clustered closely together, with their chimneys smoking. So as not to wake anyone, Inessa brought Tasha down to a slow walk as they continued through. At the back of the village was the great lodge, where they met for meetings, prayed to the gods, and held feasts.

Although, Inessa didn't pray much anymore, knowing her words fell on deaf ears. The gods were sleeping when she was born, and they slept still. What was the point?

Despite the early hour, Einar's mother stood outside of her home, hanging her rugs to be beaten later. When she caught Inessa's eye, she quickly looked away.

Inessa *knew* she believed her to be a völva. When she was a child it bothered her, but now? She laughed. Inessa was no sorceress, no prophet, nor was she divine. She was just an instrument to be wielded when Death had a need.

Völva's weren't viewed kindly in their community. The general opinion was that they were wicked, brought bad energy and spirits with them. And maybe they did, who could say? All Inessa knew was that she was no völva.

Shaking her head, she urged Tasha through the village, past the great lodge, and down the path toward the lake. Eventually the land gave way to a massive body of water. The sun kissed the top of the mountains, bathing the range in golden light, creating a purple hue to the peaks.

Inessa let Tasha inch close enough to the lake so that she could drink. Steam rose from the mare's body, reminding her how cold it actually was. She couldn't feel it, not with the furs covering her body and the warmth radiating from her horse.

She dismounted and knelt before the water, leaning forward to take a quick drink. The iciness washed over her lips and chin and energy zipped through her from the sheer coldness.

"Stars. That stings so good," Inessa said with a laugh.

The town bell rang, chasing away whatever peace she felt. She jumped to her feet, spinning on her heel. What was going on? She had just been there!

She mounted Tasha and turned her around before racing back up the path, toward the village. That bell only rang for emergencies. War, illness...Death. But she hadn't reaped in Svetl. Not in weeks.

Scraggly pine trees flashed by her as Tasha galloped up the way and when she came rushing up behind the lodge, she spied the jarl ringing the bell. His face grim, his eyes full of worry.

Inessa pulled her mare up short. She took but a moment to catch her breath. "Jarl Bodil, what it is? Has someone come for us?" Despite never seeing a true battle, she'd endured full training as a battle maiden, and her muscles yearned for a fight.

"Inessa?" The jarl shook his head. "There is no one knocking down our doors, but there is a sickness here. We woke to numerous folks fallen ill. Not just children, but adults too. Kristian, Viggo, Hans and a few more. It's odd that there are so many and with a high fever too."

Everyone had been fine at the bonfire. Perhaps it was spoiled meat?

She nodded to the jarl and waited for the villagers to spill out of their homes and congregate around him.

Soon, everyone groggily meandered their way toward the lodge, either rubbing their eyes or glancing around, questioning what the commotion was about.

From her vantage point, Inessa scanned the faces, not seeing her father among them. But he would take longer to get here than the others. They lived farther from the town center, in the woods a little ways, hidden from the main village.

With most assembled around Jarl Bodil, he spoke. "There is a sickness among us, spreading it seems. Do your due diligence. Pray to the gods, bleed the sick from your veins, and keep to Svetl. Don't venture outside of the village until we know more. Drifa will be making her rounds to the sick."

Drifa, the healer.

Inessa nudged Tasha onward, and she slowly rounded the back of the gathering, just as her father made his way toward them. Surprise filtered his expression as he walked up to her.

"What is going on?" he asked. "Not a Death?"

She didn't quite know, outside of mysterious and sudden illnesses popping up. "Some people are sick. Fevers that came out of nowhere." Inessa bit her bottom lip and cast a glance over her shoulder. "I don't want you near them if it's some plague that is about to spread through like wildfire."

He chuckled darkly. "I will be near it soon enough, if that's what you're worried about."

And she was worried. More than she cared to admit. She didn't want him ill, didn't want him catching this dreaded thing.

Father pressed his lips into a firm line. He lifted the black fur birka from his head and scratched at his dark red hair. "I hope it's not a plague," he muttered, more to himself than Inessa.

"No one wants that." Except maybe Hadeon. He'd revel in a plague as soul after soul left this world, wouldn't he? He didn't glory in the loss of life, but he never mourned, never felt anything when someone died.

He'd told that a soul passing was the equivalent to kindling being added to a fire for him. Power and energy.

"There is stew waiting for you at home. Why don't you ride back and grab some?" Her father jerked his head toward the path, trying to send her away, trying to distract her, but from what?

She opened her mouth, ready to say she wasn't hungry, but her stomach grumbled in protest. "Please," she said softly. "Come with me?" But when her father didn't look at her, she only sighed. "Don't linger long, at least."

To that, he nodded. Then she sped off, not waiting around to listen to the murmuring or fearmongering.

When she reached home, shadows gathered near the barn. She knew what it meant; Hadeon waited for her just beyond the collecting darkness.

Without so much as a glance in his direction, she rode into the paddock, hopped off her mare and tended to Tasha's needs before she considered the looming stallion behind her.

"Are you readying for them?" She peeled her eyes from the bucket of oats but didn't look at Hadeon.

Too soon to tell, but I feel the sickness in them.

She didn't want to hear him whisper to her, didn't want to see the otherness in his gaze. There was much to be done around their home still, and she opted to focus on that instead of the possibility of losing not one but many of the villagers.

"In the meantime, I've got things to do here."

Hadeon snorted and helped himself to the open stall.

Inessa left the barn. Outside, she bent to collect an arm full of logs and walked into the small cottage, her home.

Despite the sun growing in strength, a bone deep chill spread through her. Only the warmth of food would chase this kind of cold away. She walked to the hearth. Flames lapped hungrily at the charred logs. Grabbing a few from the palette, she tossed them in and then laid out the new logs in front of the fire to dry.

Flashes of the most recent lives she'd taken danced in her mind and rather than focus on them, she opened her mouth and started to sing a cheerful lullaby her mother sang to her about a boy who bartered with toys he made for food for his family.

A warrior made of gourd for a loaf of bread
And a dolly for a girl with a crown of red.
He marched to the tune of a goat's old horn,
Through fields of barley kissed by the morn.
To the mountain high and the valley low,
He danced with the frost where the fjord winds blow.

Singing brought back fond memories of the summer days when Inessa would run carefree through the stream, barefoot and as wild as a red deer. She'd pick wildflowers for her mother, who would set them on the dining table.

"Oh Mama, I wish you were here still." Inessa gathered a bowl of stew for herself and sat, staring at the empty tankard where flowers were once assembled. "At least you understand what it feels like." And sometimes, it just felt hard. A deep, tiresome ache in the center of her being weighed her down.

After eating her fill of stew, she dragged herself outside to chop more wood, because at least doing something would act as a distraction.

Five

C hopping wood couldn't erase the growing pit in Inessa's stomach. She worried for the villagers, specifically the children and her father. Winters were never easy in Svetl, but when an illness spread through like wildfire lapping at dried brush, the losses were devastating. She'd witnessed it in her earlier years as a reaper. Oh, the tears she'd cried as she coaxed soul after soul from those she knew so well.

There had been too many reapings of late, ones that brought her out of Svetl, even past Runestadt. She'd collected five in Runesby, and it seemed as though Hadeon kept pushing her farther away. He had been calling upon her even during waking hours. The increase was worrisome.

The bright spot was, Hadeon hadn't yet summoned her today.

Inessa embedded the axe in a log and turned away from her home. The cold air stung her eyes, lashed against her cheeks, but didn't chill her to the bone. She moved away from her work and headed toward the road that led to the center. Inessa couldn't get too close to anyone, but she was restless and staying put would do her no good.

Snow crunched beneath Inessa's leather ankle boots as she walked beneath the icy trees. Despite the rabbit pelt sewn to the inside, and the wool socks she wore, cold still seeped through like icy daggers. Inessa may not have felt the same as her fellow villagers, but she was still vulnerable to frost bite. She slogged through, thankful that the pine boughs shielded the path from the worst of the snowfall.

The sound of a creaking wheel caught her attention, and she turned on her heel just in time to see a shaggy brown pony, belonging to the Jorgensens, wind its way toward her. In the cart's driver's seat, Einar grinned at her and even from where she stood several yards away, she could see mischief glimmering in his dark blue eyes.

"What in the Father's name are you doing trudging through the snow?" he asked with a hint of amusement in his voice.

She could lie, but it wouldn't have been convincing and Einar would have called her out on it. "I need to do something instead of sitting at home chopping wood."

He halted the cart next to her and she stepped toward it. Some of the playfulness left his eyes. "I know. It's why I went hunting," he said, thumbing toward the wagon. "Nabbed two deer. It'll feed us for a while."

Inessa lifted onto her toes, spied two lifeless bucks in the back. "Next time take me."

"All right, Battle Maiden." He chuckled and shook his head. "Hop in, and you can help me with these two. And I'll warm you up in the meantime." Einar's gaze lifted to the road, and his expression took on a more serious note. It made her feel better knowing she wasn't alone in feeling useless. She sighed and walked around the pony, then hoisted herself onto the seat. Einar lifted a fur blanket and draped it around her shoulders, offering more warmth. She relaxed into it and leaned against him as he pushed the pony onward.

"Do you think it was the food?" Einar broke the silence that had started to settle between them.

"No, I don't."

"I don't either. We just received a fur trade from Runestadt, and I wonder if they've tainted anything. Our alliance isn't exactly the steadiest with them."

All it would take was a whisper of wrongdoing among the villagers and Jarl Bodil would ready the warriors for battle.

"I don't think it's them, and if it was, I don't think it was intentional." Something niggled at her, telling her that it wasn't them. Still, she didn't exactly trust their neighbors.

"Mother says the sickness will take over the village," he said.

It wouldn't take much. Svetl was less than two hundred people.

Especially in the middle of winter.

Eventually, the woods gave way to the village and Einar turned left, letting the pony trot toward the back of his family's log home. He halted at the small lean-to with a paddock and quickly untacked the shaggy equine before setting it loose to eat some fresh hay.

Inessa hopped out and lifted the wagon, dragging it toward the deer hoist. Four large tree limbs created a sturdy support system, while another ran across the top, where the deer would hang so they could begin dressing it.

"Yeah, yeah, we know you're strong." Einar batted her

out of the way playfully and hauled the cart over. He made quick work of tying one buck up. "Now, let's do some good."

Inessa nodded and pulled a blade free from her boot, ready to welcome this productive destruction with a good friend.

As the last dregs of the sun faded, the villagers who were able lit torches outside of their homes to shed light on their settlement.

"I should get home. Who knows how long we have before the next storm." She bent down, wiping her blade clean in the snow.

Inessa.

Hadeon's voice raked across her mind. His presence wrapped around her like a stifling shroud of smoke.

She needed to leave at once. Death was imminent for someone.

"I'll drop you off. Let me hitch Shaggy." Einar cleaned his knife and started toward the pony's paddock.

"No!" She bit her bottom lip, trying to calm her voice. It wasn't him; it was knowing that someone, or *someones*, was close to Death's door. "No, it's okay. Get food to those who need it. I know my way back home." Not that she would make it that far.

"Good night, Inessa." Einar caught her eye and offered a smile.

"Take care of yourself, Einar." With that, she rounded his property and picked up the trail that led to her home, knowing she'd never reach it before Hadeon found her.

Shadows seemed to collect themselves and Hadeon took shape, trotting toward her. Inessa turned to the side as he approached, reached for his mane and yanked herself astride him. He didn't so much as pause in his gait before trotting back through the village.

Inessa passed row after row of log homes until she reached the very end, closest to the Great Lodge. The scent of herbs permeated the air, most likely being burned to stave off the sickness. Peppermint, sage, and rosemary tickled Inessa's nose.

She dismounted Hadeon and stared at the wooden door before her. "Viggo," she whispered, knowing this was the home of the little boy Vanja had been playing with just the other day at the bonfire.

Inessa stepped forward, climbing the stairs that led to the door and then pushing it open. Sweat collected on her brow. It was overly warm inside, and she wondered if that was for the boy's benefit.

Across the room was a large hearth with a chimney that was easily half the size of the home itself. To her immediate left and right doors opened to other rooms. When she stopped and listened, she heard the rattling breaths of Viggo.

She frowned. *I'm sorry, little one.*

A tug. A pull to the left and she entered the boy's room. The familiar pulsing of white light clung to Viggo, beckoning Inessa forward.

She hovered over him, taking in his gray complexion that was normally pink and full of life. His curly mop of brown hair was damp with fever. Watching the raspy, pull of breath he took, she thought there was no way this was simply bad meat.

His soul oozed from his body before she had the chance to coax it from him. It wound around her arm gently, as if on some level he knew her still.

"May the Great Stallion guide you to the Hall," Inessa

35

whispered, pulling his fur blankets up a fraction more. He wouldn't feel the cold any longer, but it was the least she could do.

The soul snaked its way upward, stretching until it was as taught as a bow string and as slender as one too. Then, in a blink, it burst into nothingness.

When it was done, Inessa was exhausted.

"Are we done?" she whispered to Hadeon, who would hear her no matter his location.

"For tonight."

She quickly left the home, hopped on Hadeon's back, and they sped toward her home. The night was early, earlier than usual and she needed to sleep, because tomorrow would surely be long.

When they arrived, she slid from his back. Inessa didn't spare him a glance as she strode forward and opened the door to their home.

Father sat at the dining table in front of the hearth, eating a portion of bread.

In that moment of silence, they shared an understanding. Perhaps it was a look in her eye. Perhaps it was how she held herself. But all he did was nod his head, because he knew what had been done.

"I need sleep," she murmured.

"I won't stop you, my girl. I'll feed the fire before I nod off."

Inessa turned toward her small room, just large enough for her sleeping pallet. Furs hung around the window to block the harsh winds and drafts. Next to it, a thin wardrobe held her hangeroks.

She inched forward, stripping free of her fur coat and

hung it on the wall. She stripped until only her woolen shift fell about her calves, then climbed beneath the heavy weight of her blankets.

Inessa slept for now, for come morning the bell would toll.

Six

Inessa woke with a start as the town-center bell tolled. With each toll it cried, *Death, Death, one of ours has fallen.* She scrubbed her eyes, then looked out the window as if she could discern what time it was but the window was darkened to blot out any light. Was the sun up yet? She cast her gaze toward her doorway and saw the soft light of morning splashing on the floor.

She groaned and slid out of bed, her bare feet touching the chilled floor.

Inessa swore under her breath and shuffled toward her wardrobe. She tossed open the doors and pulled out fresh stockings and a blue hangerok.

She quickly dressed and grabbed her fur coat as she walked out into the shared living space. Her father wasn't sitting at the table, staring into the hearth's flames like usual. This didn't surprise her; he'd known she had reaped and knew to be prepared.

As the undertaker, it was her father's turn to take care of things. He would help the Tolunson family clean and prepare the boy for the afterlife, dress him in his best clothes, bind his body in cotton, then gift him a weapon so that he would be seen as strong as he entered the heavens.

After Father loaded the boy into the wagon came the village walk to the lake. Little Viggo would be set ablaze, so that the gods may greet him swiftly.

A feast would be had in his family's honor too.

Inessa shrugged her fur coat on. It was time to join her community.

As Inessa stepped into the village clearing, she heard the Death song long before she zeroed in on Viggo's mother. They'd already traveled from their home and wove their way up this far. The trek was part of the process, allowing each villager to offer their condolences along the way.

Dressed in black furs, Viggo's mother and her husband led the procession, snaking around the town center and back toward the lake.

Inessa bowed her head as they walked past, then stepped in behind the growing group of followers. She hummed the melody, low and mournful, just as the others did.

Let Death fall like winter's breath,
Sweeping o'er the fields of Death.
The brave are crowned, their names resound,
The weak are mourned, their solace found.
Ashes kiss the trembling lake,
Blood of kin feeds the roots that wake.
The heavens call with horns of light,
Through shadowed vale and endless night.

Inessa didn't bother searching for her father; he'd be with Viggo at the pyre near the water. Father would prepare the pyre, and the village would sing until the fire released the soul. These were ceremonial rituals in Svetl.

When Inessa was young, she believed in their traditions, but when Hadeon claimed her, she knew differently. The soul left the body upon one's last breath, and when she'd said as much to her father, he'd sighed, then told her, "Let them grieve as they may. If it comforts them, let them believe, Inessa. We all deserve that."

She wound her way through the village, and someone grabbed her hand, squeezing it. Inessa peered up to see Einar, offering her a small, sad smile.

Inessa took comfort in his presence, squeezing his hand in return.

By the time her boots crunched on the forest floor, there was a succession of individuals behind them, humming and swaying as they bobbed through the woods.

Snow flurries tickled and stung her face as they trod down the bridle path that gave way to the Ljus Lake. Beneath dark clouds, the water appeared dark, like obsidian, but the surface glittered still, reminding Inessa of the depth of Hadeon's eyes.

The villagers fanned out along the shore, and just like that, the humming ceased. Inessa stepped closer toward the bank of the lake to better see, and Einar hovered behind her.

Jarl Bodil stepped forward. The proud wolf hood of his fur coat sat atop his head, and he stared up at the sky.

"Today, we give back Viggo Tolunson. While we grieve, he shall rejoice in the presence of the Great Ones! And for that, we will celebrate too." He bowed his head to Viggo's parents, then bent down and took a flint from his pocket.

He struck it until it sparked, and the small embers caught on the dried swath of linen wrapped around a bundle of sticks.

The flames lapped hungrily at the kindling, and he calmly picked the torch up before walking it toward Viggo's father. "May he honor you in the afterlife," Jarl Bodil said sadly and backed away from the family.

Together, Viggo's parents walked toward the awaiting pyre as it bobbed in the water, and for a moment, they paused, then threw the torch on the raft. The ravenous flames blazed, and Inessa's father pushed the raft away from the shore.

Viggo's mother fell to her knees, crying as her only son drifted farther and farther away.

Inessa looked away and swallowed roughly, clenching her teeth as the woman wailed in misery. A pang of regret cracked the wall she'd erected around her heart, the one she'd raised to shield herself from the hurt and anguish that came with each reaping.

Death is part of living, Inessa.

The gravelly voice resounded in her mind, and she looked up to see Hadeon standing by her father. His proud neck arched, crimped mane swaying wildly. His eyes, though, were locked onto her.

Death is par for the course. Do not mourn for them.

Hadeon repeated, having told her this long ago, when she'd reaped her first soul.

How could she not grieve? She was human and Death, no matter how many times she faced it, was always sad. An entity like Death couldn't understand the sorrow of the living.

She tore her gaze away and stared down at the frozen

mud, waiting until the Tolunsons walked away from the embankment.

Inessa glanced at Viggo's mother, her face red from crying and her shoulders still shaking. The villagers chanted the song in a throaty growl, stomping their feet to usher Viggo's soul into the afterlife.

Jarl Bodil withdrew the horn that dangled from his hip and blew into it. He bellowed and then cried out to the heavens, a foreboding roar that might have awakened the Great Ones.

Inessa growled along with the other villagers and beat on her chest, hoping their gods would remain asleep. And if they should wake, perhaps break their cycle of being merciless.

She sucked in a ragged breath, knowing it was a foolish thought. For the Great Ones never listened, but it felt good, even for just a moment, to let her frustrations out and blend in with the cries of the other villagers.

"Inessa?" Einar asked, standing beside her.

She turned to face him. Concern rumpled his brow and pinched his lips.

"I'm all right." And she would be, as soon as she mended that crack in her composure. Inessa swiped her cheek, flicking away a single tear. The only one she would allow herself to cry.

Einar's mother stepped toward them, sorrow etched on her features. A new paleness joined her already fair complexion, but when the woman realized it was Inessa, her brows furrowed, and she muttered a warding. "Stay away from her," she said to her son, none too quietly.

"Mother, Inessa isn't a völva," Einar said, with a hint of a laugh. "And now isn't the time for your superstitions."

She most certainly wasn't a witch.

"No," his mother said, looking straight at Inessa. "She's Death touched. Her whole family is." Her gaze went to Hadeon and Inessa thought she saw fear warp her features. Yet when the woman looked back at her, her eyes had hardened already.

If Inessa were the betting sort, she would place her finest pelt on Einar's mother not knowing just how touched by Death Inessa really was.

But weren't they all?

Seven

It was late into the night when Viggo's send-off ended, and Inessa wasn't certain how she had managed walking home. She paused at her modest door, waiting to see if Hadeon thrashed in the barn, waiting to see if he had another demand for her. He didn't make a sound, so she went inside.

Thankfully, she'd eaten some offerings at the ceremony, which meant she didn't need to devour bread before dragging herself to bed.

She pried her boots off and sat them before the hearth, then added more logs to the fire. It'd do no good if the went out entirely, especially with the threat of more snow.

When she peeled the last fur layer off and hung it from a wooden rack near the door, she walked toward the bedrooms and paused just outside her father's. It was dark, and since there was little moonlight, she could scarcely see his form beneath the white fur blanket.

Inessa frowned. Her father had been withdrawn as of late, and while it was coming up on the anniversary of her mother's Death, she feared Hadeon would come for him soon. If that were the case, how could she fight it?

Putting the thought from her mind, she turned away from his sleeping form and went to her room. She entered her small quarters and undressed, then slid into bed. There wasn't much she held dear, save for a twine necklace that hung on the wall above her bed. It had belonged to her mother, a small flower pendant she had carved out of wood.

"Good night, Mama," she whispered. Inessa kissed her fingers, then touched the wooden trinket.

She buried herself beneath the blankets, closed her eyes, and willed herself to sleep.

Get up.

The voice stirred her, but she didn't open her eyes. She burrowed her nose into her down pillow and willed herself into sleep once more.

It is time we go. Now.

Hadeon's voice held a stern demand and while Inessa wanted to ignore it, she felt his words wash over her and prick at her muscles. If she dallied any longer her body would rise of its own accord, compelled by Hadeon's force. Inessa gritted her teeth and slid from her bed. She crossed the small room and lifted the fur away from the window. The moon was out, which meant the heavy snow clouds had passed, but she'd likely only had two hours of sleep.

She loosed a breath and as her eyes refocused on the window, Hadeon appeared. If it hadn't been for the moonlight, she wouldn't have made out his appearance, but there he stood, a majestic stallion with a sleek black coat and fiery eyes, looming near the side of the house with an air of command.

As if sensing her hesitation, the horse snorted impatiently and pawed at the ground with a powerful hoof. His gaze bore into hers, demanding compliance. Normally, she wouldn't pause, but the reapings were growing closer together, the fevers worsening, the sickness spreading fast.

Viggo had just been the night prior, and before that, another in the neighboring village.

"The fevers are spreading, aren't they?" she asked, dressing as quickly as possible.

"Yes. Now let us go."

And as he spun away from the window, the tether that bound them together grew so taut that the breath left her lungs. She fell to the floor. Pain slithered from her heart, toward her extremities, as if she touched flames. She clenched her teeth so tightly that she thought they'd crack.

A sharp command from Hadeon required no words.

His demand echoed in her mind, soul, and body like a haunting refrain. He released a low nicker, sounding more equine than spectral.

She wasn't denying him. She was merely curious, but Hadeon didn't always understand or he *care* to understand human curiosity.

Forcing herself to rise, Inessa strode toward the rack in her room and took up the black fur coat. Once fully dressed, she left her room and paused by the door. The urge to kiss her father rose within her, not because she'd never see him again. She feared that soon he'd be tainted too.

With a sigh, she left the warmth of her home and strode across the front yard to the awaiting stallion.

The moon cast an eerie glow over the woodlands that

surrounded her home, lending the frostbitten trees a ghostly appearance.

Snow crunched beneath her boots as she walked to Hadeon. He wore no saddle. It was just as well. She didn't need one, not when she'd grown up on horseback.

"Where to this time?" she finally asked.

We'll remain in Runestadt.

She rubbed between her eyes and sighed. The sickness was spreading. How far would it go? Across the continent?

Just another dead mortal. That was likely all Hadeon thought of the losses. It was his role in life, after all.

Hadeon halted in front of a desolate clearing. It was here that Inessa's task awaited her, a grim duty. She slid from Hadeon's back and stared at the small hut. She knew who she had come for.

Embla. One of Svetl's midwives. She had moved to Runestadt when her husband died and had chosen to live with her daughter in what Inessa deemed enemy territory. Still, the irony wasn't lost on Inessa, for this woman had brought her into the world, and now Inessa was taking her out of it.

Long ago, Inessa had asked Hadeon what people saw when she stepped before them. Did they see her? Would they know she came for them?

Hadeon had told her they saw what they wanted, but they'd never truly see her.

Grimacing, she stepped forward. She knew what she had to do, but the thought of it made her stomach churn.

As she readied to open the door, the hair on her neck rose. She spun around, eyes wide.

Wait.

There! The same presence she had felt before. Her eyes

darted to Hadeon who looked as though he were standing on the tips of his hooves; he was so high strung. His nostrils flared and the whites of his eyes showed.

What in the Great Ones was going on? Hadeon frightened? Or in the very least alarmed? She turned in a circle, watching and waiting.

Hadeon's ears swiveled. *We should leave now.*

Inessa couldn't hear what he did, but she *felt* something —someone. *No, no. It's impossible.* Only animals could sense her, see her, and Hadeon.

As she turned, she scanned the tree line, looking for twitching branches, or the gleam of an eye.

Then, she spotted them.

Inessa's heart raced as she homed in on the figure. If she hadn't been looking for them, their white pelts would have blended in with the freshly fallen snow. But there, stepping from the tree line, was a large, shrouded figure walking toward her. And not just heading her way, but truly looking at her. This person *saw* her.

"Stop!" she hissed and held her hand out. "Who are you?" They halted, clearly hearing her as well. Disbelief swirled through her mind, like a whirlwind. How could they hear her, let alone see her?

"I mean no harm," came the smooth tones of a man. His accent was slightly different. Every village had their own dialect, but she recognized the lilting tones of a local. The man pushed his white hood down to his shoulders. He had blond hair kept in tidy braids, and a short pale beard, but beyond that, she couldn't discern his features.

Get on, *girl.* Something akin to fear had crept into Hadeon's tone.

Inessa's gaze narrowed on him. Why fear? In all her years

she'd never seen him frightened. Inessa stepped closer to him, reaching for his mane. She readied to mount, despite wanting to plant her foot and see who this man was, but Hadeon's words were always a command.

"Wait," the white wolf of a man said, holding out his hand.

His presence sent a chill down her spine, and yet his words seemed to cut through Hadeon's ability to compel her. She set her foot in the snow and faced him once again.

Was he more powerful than Hadeon? A god perhaps.

"How can you see me?" Inessa breathed out.

He is no one to linger for. Get on, Inessa. We must leave. Hadeon shoved at her with his muzzle, forcing her into his side.

"And why are you following me? It was you by the lake." She assumed. The feeling prickling at her skin now, she had felt there.

Inessa's gaze flicked from Hadeon to the stranger. He stepped into clear view, and she noted the smile playing at the corner of his lips. Open, inviting, warm even. He stepped closer.

"I've been watching you and taking note of the reap-ings," he replied in a calm tone.

Hadeon swung around, arching his neck as the man approached. Inessa had never seen him act this way before. He snorted, and his breath vaporized like smoke.

"You shouldn't be here," Inessa warned the man and sidestepped behind Hadeon. If he was out of sorts, she was convinced there was even more reason to flee.

"I'm exactly where I need to be," he replied, cryptically. His voice sounded so smooth, so soothing.

Inessa, get on!

She rushed toward Hadeon. However, the man moved forward, and the horse bolted to the side, away from him, as if his very touch would sear him.

The man held no weapon except for his disarming smile. "Your voice holds no thrall over me, Death" he said to the horse, advancing with slow, deliberate steps. His movements reminded Inessa of a grown man approaching a fearful child. "I just want to talk, Hadeon."

Cold speared its way through her. How in the Great Halls did he know Hadeon's name? Inessa's instincts screamed at her to flee, but curiosity won over.

This man seemed familiar, as if she'd seen him before. Yet, that did nothing to soothe her racing heart. "Talking is all you're doing. You're not supplying any answers." Inessa warred over whether she should summon her sword, but the stranger hadn't yet posed an actual threat to her.

Hadeon couldn't die so in theory he had nothing to fear.

Run, Inessa, run! The horse's voice echoed in her mind, a command urging her to escape.

"You don't have to go, Inessa," the man said. This time, it dawned on her that he could *hear* Hadeon too. For the man knew her name and knew that he'd instructed her to run.

Flee, Inessa. Before it's too late! Hadeon shouted frantically, then bolted.

Eight

She had a choice, run into the night as Death commanded, or stay and figure out who the man was. If he chose to lure her into a fight, she would prove to him that she wasn't easy prey. She had trained as a battle maiden, spent hours building muscle, both physical and mental. He would regret it.

"At least one of you has sense," the man said softly. "If you won't hear me out, then at least watch." He brushed past her, toward Embla's home and Inessa's breath caught.

Where had Hadeon gone?

Fear crept up her spine. "Wait. Don't step any closer to that door." She didn't know him and therefore didn't trust his intentions. While she may have been ready to reap Embla moments ago, she certainly didn't want someone else doing her job.

The blond male shot her a look. "You won't be able to stop me."

That rankled her. She gritted her teeth, fighting the urge to summon the blade she rarely ever used.

"Summon your sword if you must, but then at least follow me inside." He sounded exhausted, as if she were trying his patience.

The audacity.

Inessa flexed her fingers and as she did a spectral light stemmed from her wrist and took shape. Soon a glimmering broad sword formed in her grip, and though it was not steel, it held the force of it. The weapon was not meant for graceful thrusts, but rather for hacking.

One successful blow and any opponent's soul would be taken. And if this man was presenting himself as an enemy, he was going to venture to the Great Hall soon.

The stranger grunted at her.

She followed him to the door and when he pushed inside, she was close on his heels. One wrong move and she would strike him down.

"What is your name?" she asked coolly, leveling him with a hard look as she followed his every move.

He turned, his lips pursed in mild amusement as if he thought her nothing more than a child playing with a wooden sword. She'd have to make him reconsider that smirk.

"Stellan," she said, then headed down a hall toward, what she assumed were, the modest bedrooms.

The name tickled her memory. She'd heard that name, seen his face, but from where? Not from Svetl.

She scrunched her nose and glanced around Embla's small room, decorated sparsely with a bed and dresser against the wall. The one extravagance—a woven blanket hung above the bed. Embla had worked all of one summer making it. Inessa recalled the old woman's fingers weaving cobalt blue, gold, and ivories into Svetlian glyphs honoring Gyda. Bold of her to showcase them on her walls in Runestadt.

She curled her lip and glanced up at the man. "Why come here?" Inessa bit out and as Stellan edged closer to Embla's bed, her rasping breaths seemed to worsen. Inessa swore under her breath and lifted her sword to the nape of his neck. "Not an inch closer," she growled.

He did not listen. Instead, his fingertips glowed a soft gold. Strands of light streamed from him, circling into a knotted design that Inessa knew well—a symbol of life.

The knot floated toward Embla's brow and settled onto her forehead. It glowed for a moment, pulsed, then faded ever so slightly.

In all her sixteen years of reaping, she'd never seen anything like it. Fascinated and slightly mortified, Inessa pressed her blade against Stellan's neck. "What was that?" she hissed, then corrected herself. "What are you?" Although the question dripped from her like venom, she already had an idea of the answer.

A lifebringer. The antithesis to her deathbringing abilities.

Hadeon had told her about them and had grown agitated with her many questions. So she'd never asked again, and she assumed there hadn't been a lifebringer since she'd been reaping without incident until now.

Stellan grew eerily still. "Inessa, I am not a threat to you." He pointed down at Embla. "She cannot be reaped, unless her soul has given up the fight." He shook his head. "And her fight is not yet done."

Her sword flickered away, and she dropped her hand, staring dumbfoundedly at him. Hadeon had never mentioned that part of a lifebringer's abilities—seeing when a soul's fight was over.

A new flood of questions entered her mind. Did a lifebringer's mark upset the balance when placed on a soul that was meant to be reaped? Had there been a lifebringer when her mother was alive? And if so, could she have been saved from her sickness?

"Lifebringer," she finally said.

He spun and looked at her. Despite the darkness, she could see his glacier blue eyes and the sincerity they held within them. Stellan stood a full head taller than her, and it finally dawned on her where she recognized him from.

Inessa had seen him, shook hands with him at the peace ceremony. He had smiled at her! Their two communities may have struck a shaky new alliance, still she didn't trust them. She stepped backward, brows furrowing. "You're the jarl of Runestadt's son."

Had he been a lifebringer even then?

She brought her hands to her eyes and rubbed them. "How long?" she whispered.

"Come with me," Stellan said, offering his hand to her.

"No." She backed farther away from him, not out of fear, but disbelief and disgust. Hlíf, the spirit of Life, would embody someone from Runestadt?

"Leave me alone and leave Svetl." She turned on her heel and walked out of the house. Hadeon materialized before her. She grabbed a hold of his mane and pulled herself up.

Stellan jogged outside. "I can't leave, Inessa!" He called to her but she didn't dare peer over her shoulder.

She spurred Hadeon on. His hooves struck the ground, churning up snow and ice in their wake. Inessa's heart raced so violently that her chest ached. "Did you know a lifebringer was around?"

Silence greeted her. She squeezed his coarse strands of hair and nearly screamed as anger bubbled up inside of her.

When they arrived home, she dismounted. Hadeon walked toward the barn, but she barred his path. She was tired of his tangled web of secrets. He'd always picked and chosen what information she was privy to. Hadeon regarded her with his piercing gaze and his bottom lip twitched as he seemed to weigh her words. And then, with a voice like thunder rolling across the sky, he spoke. *I had a suspicion. I felt the presence of Hlíf but didn't think she would summon a lifebringer. There hasn't been one in nearly a hundred years.*

The ground seemed to shift beneath her. "What? Then how are life and Death balanced?" she whispered and closed the distance between them. She placed her hand on his nose and Hadeon lowered his head further.

Because the reapers are doing as they must.

"And so is the lifebringer. If Stellan stopped me, it was for a reason." Doubt flared to life in her. Hadeon had never killed someone, as far as she knew. But he was an ancient being who thought and felt little of mortal life, who was to say he never had?

Hadeon jerked his head away from her and continued down the beaten path to the barn. She followed him, blinking as she entered the dark structure. Tasha whinnied and Inessa scooped a handful of oats to feed her.

You know the consequences of denying me.

She paused and curled her fingers into her palms. "Death."

Her heart hammered in her chest. The simple word

tasted bitter to her and for a moment, she thought, maybe, he would correct her, but Hadeon snorted.

Death.

Inessa felt ill. Had her mother disobeyed Hadeon's orders all those years ago? She was afraid to ask. Afraid that if she knew, she'd die too.

Shadows stretched along the walls as Hadeon entered a stall. His form lost some of its solidity, and she wasn't certain if her eyes played tricks on her or if he faded into the darkness.

"What am I supposed to do to combat him? I've never faced a lifebringer before." Annoyance crept into her tone as she inched forward.

Whatever you must, he said, then lowered his voice and added, *your life depends on it.*

Inessa's ears rang, forcing her to sit in the mound of hay behind her. She pressed her fingers to her eyes, willing the buzzing from her ears to stop. She thought about her mother again and gritted her teeth. Could, or would, he snuff out her life so easily? She shot up from the hay and stormed out of the bard, anger propelling her forward. For only one thing was clear.

Hadeon had just threatened her.

Nine

In all of her adult years, Inessa had never considered facing a lifebringer. A hundred years since the last one? What had happened to them?

Inessa stopped in her tracks and turned toward the barn. The open doors looked more like a gaping, black maw. From where she stood, she couldn't see the stalls.

She huffed a breath and strode toward the structure again, wanting to force more answers from the horse. "Hadeon—"

Except, he wasn't there. At least, not in horse form. She peered up at the eaves, wondering if any of the shadows belonged to him.

"What am I supposed to do if he marks them?" she muttered, not really expecting an answer.

Avoid the lifebringer. Hadeon's voice rolled through her mind despite his solid form not being present.

He made it seem so simple. How was she to win against a being immune to her abilities? A lifebringer and reaper canceled out one another's abilities. She could not reap his soul, and he could not save hers. At least that's how the old stories went.

Continue to reap, Inessa. Be clever about it.

Hadeon's insistence on harvesting souls to maintain balance lingered like a haunting melody. Though she warred with the idea, because her life depended on it.

With one last glare toward the beams in the barn, Inessa left and walked back to the comfort of the house.

Glowing embers in the hearth offered little light or warmth. She strode forward and grabbed a few logs to add on.

"Long night?" Father's voice cut through the relative silence.

She bolted upright, nearly whacking her head on the mantle.

"You could say that," she said as she walked toward the table and plopped down in a chair.

Her father yawned, scratching his neck as he crossed the room to join her. "Want to talk about it?"

No. "Yes." Inessa combed her fingers through her hair. Frozen strands had tangled together. She was a mess inside and out.

"Will the bell toll?" he asked, but there was little question in his tone. He had always been perceptive, able to sense when something troubled her, even when she tried to hide it.

"There was no reaping," she replied and shrugged off the black furs, then shifted so she could tuck the coat over the back of the chair.

"Oh..." Now he sounded quite puzzled. "Is everything—"

"A complication." She chewed her bottom lip. Since her mother had been a reaper, he knew the innerworkings of this life, but there hadn't been a lifebringer then. What would he even know about them besides what every other villager knew?

"Are you hungry?"

"I'm so hungry."

"Let me see what I can do about that," her father said with a chuckle and stood from the table. Gone was his grogginess as he set about making her a quick meal.

He grabbed a few eggs from a bowl and a bit of bacon from the cellar. Before long, the aroma of pork fat filled the room. Once the cooking was done, he set a plate before her with a hunk of bread.

She grabbed a piece of the bread and folded it, then used it to spoon up the meal. She moaned as the flavors hit her tongue.

"You know," her father said, "I saw Einar on my walk earlier and he said the fever is spreading. Not just in Svetl but in the neighboring villages too. Runestadt, Hrautsby..." He ticked them off on his fingers.

Inessa's chewing slowed. She had half hoped she could get through the meal without talking more on the matter. "I noticed." She placed a small piece of bread in her mouth. "It only makes sense since the fever is spreading and worsening."

She savored a bite of the pork. "And you know about the balance with Life and Death? How there can sometimes be a lightbringer?"

Father sat down, his brows rumpling in confusion. "But there hasn't been one—"

"Since before mama. Except there is one now."

Father's eyes widened, but he didn't say a word. Inessa crammed another bite of food into her mouth. "Hadeon says the balance is being threatened, and if I don't continue to reap, he'll—"

"He will." Father let out a shaky sigh and dragged his hand down his face. "He will most certainly take your life. When he claims you as maiden, he also claims your soul. You know that."

Inessa did know, all too well. She placed her empty bowl down. The food sat heavily in her belly, threatening to turn sour.

He nodded slowly, pressing his lips together as he looked toward the ceiling. "Your mother didn't want to reap anymore. She had grown tired of it and wanted to embrace life, *your* life."

Every time Inessa recalled moments with her mother, they were nothing but goodness, full of life and joy. Try as she may, she couldn't see the exhaustion or frustration her mother might have felt.

She rubbed at her chest, loathing the ache there.

"Hadeon warned her, and she ignored him. In the end, he took what was his." He swore beneath his breath. "It could have been quick, but he wanted to make a point, you know? I don't think your mother believed he would do it. She knew if anything happened to her, you were the next one." He shook his head. "I don't understand her reasoning, honestly."

A chill ran along her flesh, and she shivered at the revelation. Inessa's gaze lingered on the table, and it was the sting of tears that made her look away. Her father leaned forward, reached for her hand, and took it in his calloused palm. "Continue to reap. I cannot bear to lose you."

Inwardly, she flinched. Her life wasn't more important than her neighbors, or the village itself. She stood and closed the distance between them, then embraced her father. "I'm not going anywhere. Not yet." Inessa forced a smile and leaned down to brush a kiss against his dark red hair.

INESSA SAT ON A LOG IN FRONT OF LJUS LAKE, watching as the snow geese swam and dove beneath the water's surface. Her father had taken Tasha and their wagon, which meant Inessa had to trek through the ice on foot. Not that she minded. The journey was enough to wake her.

Hadeon was as frigid as Ljus Lake and as unyielding as the Icefell mountains.

But he was exactly who and what he was: Death.

Still. If the fevers were spreading, did that mean he was attempting to tip the balance? Life hadn't needed a servant for over a century.

Inessa stared at the watery graveyard. A half-melted layer of ice covered the top of the water. A long-tailed duck swooped down, landed on top of it, and the ice shattered. The waterfowl settled into the coldness.

She sucked in her bottom lip and reached out, her fingers barely touching the surface.

A twig snapped nearby, and she turned her ear toward the side of the embankment, curious as to who or what approached. She expected a squirrel or perhaps a fox rooting around for food. What she didn't expect was the man staring back at her..

Stellan.

The lifebringer.

She quickly rose to her feet, heart thumping wildly in her ears.

"Inessa," he said in a voice that warmed her bones.

His tone had a comforting effect on her, so did his smile. Too bad he was from Runestadt.

"Please, let me talk." He held his hand out in a placating gesture. "I want to explain things." He wore a tan hide, likely that of an elk, with no cap, and she could see the tips of his ears tinted red.

Inessa eyed him warily as he drew closer, but she didn't say a word, not until he stood mere feet from her.

"Go on." She clenched her teeth. She wanted answers, and if he was willing to give them to her...

Stellan's shoulders relaxed, and he lowered his hands to his side. "Do you think you can help me?" His eyes softened as he studied her.

"Help you what?" she asked incredulously. "How am I supposed to help you? I should be asking you to help me."

Stellan's brows pinched. "What do you mean?"

"You're a lifebringer, which means you'll be marking souls I'm meant to take. If I don't reap, I will die." Inessa inhaled sharply, her brows narrowing. In the daylight, Stellan was rather beautiful in a rugged manner—chiseled jaw, sharp nose, and eyes that held so much kindness and mirth within them. "You're Kveld's son?" She'd seen Kveld once. A mountain of a man, with eyes full of laughter, and hair a ghostly shade of blond. Now that she was scrutinizing Stellan, she could see the resemblance.

Stellan cocked his head. "I am, but—" He squatted beside her and his expression darkened a fraction. "He'll kill you if you don't reap?"

She laughed, mirthlessly. "More like turn my soul to dust. I was dead the moment he claimed me."

Something akin to anger flashed in his gaze.

"Why are you a lifebringer, son of Kveld?" she asked.

"I don't know," he supplied and shrugged. "One day I was me, just the son of Kveld, and the next day I woke to a white wolf looming over me." He rubbed the back of his neck, confusion rumpling his brow. "At first, I thought I was dreaming, because she was speaking to me. In here," he said, pointing to his temple. "But she wouldn't fade no matter how much I pinched myself."

Hlíf. The beautiful white wolf. Inessa had never seen her, but she had heard about her through village stories. Although, the villagers never called her by name, they referred to her only as the Great Wolf.

She guided souls to the Great Hall.

Hadeon was never mentioned in scrolls or lore in the way that Inessa knew him as the horse. He always appeared as a shadowed figure, sometimes hooded, and other times as a skeletal being.

"Why would Hlíf pick you?" Inessa shot him a look. "Your village nearly decimated mine."

A look of pain passed over Stellan's features. "Inessa, I never wanted that. And neither did most of the village. It was an old grudge my father had with your jarl."

While the discussion about grudges and warring villages should have been a welcome distraction, it was beside the point.

Inessa rubbed her temples and sighed. "When did you wake to Hlíf?" Had it been as long as the peace ceremony? No. It couldn't have been. Hadeon would have sensed him, right?

"Three days ago."

Ten

Three *days ago.* He'd been a lifebringer for three bloody days? A lifebringer hadn't been around for nearly one hundred years and then all of a sudden one awakened three days ago. She counted backward and the only clue she could find as to why this might happen was the increased number of illnesses. Did that mean Death was trying to tip the scale? Unbalance the give and take of the earthly plains?

Inessa glanced at Stellan, still wondering why Hlíf would choose him as her enemy. She shook her head and flexed her fingers, trying to keep from forming fists.

"Hlíf told me her fears. She believes you'll reap the mountain villages to near extinction and will leave it in ruins."

Inessa's heart roared in her ears. She stared hard at him, as if she hadn't heard what he had just said. As if she didn't reek of guilt—past and future. But reaping the villages out of existence? Surely Hadeon would never. "I haven't—" Lie. If Hadeon commanded it, so it would be.

She stopped herself before the inevitably weak argument ensued.

"I don't know what I'm supposed to do." He inched forward, pausing as Inessa straightened.

She eyed him, then looked away at the lake. "Shouldn't Hlíf be telling you?"

He snorted. "Yes, and she is, but... Did you know what to do right from the beginning?"

Inessa closed her eyes and remembered the first time she reaped. She had only been twelve, and she stood on shaking legs as she approached a sleeping old woman—Kassia. She had been the village's healer and had lived a long life.

Kassia lay bundled under a heap of furs. Her breathing had slowed, the color from her aged cheeks had turned gray. Life seeped from her whether Inessa willed it to or not.

Tears had stung Inessa's eyes, her chest squeezed tight as Hadeon's impatient guidance led her through the steps.

"No," she said tightly.

Stellan reached out, and this time, he grabbed her by the hand and squeezed gently. His warmth spread through her, and t he look in his eyes was so sincere that she swallowed the lump that grew in her throat.

He was touching her.

As far as she knew, Hlíf and Hadeon could never touch. If they did, it would weaken them both, but Stellan's touch didn't weaken her. No power surged, no repulsion shot up her arm. It almost felt normal.

"You may be new, but I'm certain Hlíf is helping you." Hadeon may have wanted her to perform tasks, but he wasn't patient, and he wasn't always gentle. He'd rushed her through, barking at her as she'd reaped Kassia. He had even nipped at her when she fled the house in tears.

"The issue here is, strong souls are falling ill. If both the weak and strong fall, there will be no one left."

Beneath his hand, her skin tingled, feeling as if he'd wrapped her in a furs in front of the hearth. Or tucked her safely beneath her blankets at home. His touch chased away the chill in her bones, tempting her to lean closer.

Instead she yanked her hand away and tucked it into her lap. She still didn't trust him, didn't want to believe he wasn't twisting the truth in some way. Yet she knew better; a lifebringer hadn't been suddenly made for no reason.

"Come with me to Runestadt. Come see that I speak the truth."

She didn't have to go. She knew what the village held. Well, not in depth, but she knew there was sickness there, just as there was in Svetl. In the other surrounding villages too.

"Why aren't you there already? Why aren't you healing your people?" She hissed as she recalled the mark he'd made on Embla. "You shouldn't be here." Inessa stood and every muscle in her body tensed.

"What?" Confusion and alarm registered on his features. He rose and stared down at her. "Inessa—"

"No, if what you say is true, you shouldn't be here. You should be home, healing your people. You are Kveld's son, then do as he would and take care of Runestadt." She carefully sidestepped the log behind her and cradled the hand that he'd held. It still radiated with the heat he'd given her.

"I don't want to fight you, Inessa, but if you reap anymore souls in Svetl, or elsewhere, I must do as I'm bid. Hlíf will force me to stop you." A deep sadness wilted his gaze, and he bit his bottom lip. "Be well." He turned and walked away, back toward the edge of the forest.

Great Ones. She felt awful, as if she'd just kicked a pup to the bushes.

How dare he. How dare he make her...feel.

~

FATHER SAT IN FRONT OF A SMALL FIRE OUTSIDE their home, whittling at a chunk of wood. The steady rhythm of his blade chipped away bark and fiber and blended with that of the surrounding wildlife. An owl hooted, the low tune keeping the same tempo as the *shuck-shuck-shucking*.

If Inessa could focus on her father's simple, soothing task, then perhaps she could blot out everything screaming in her head.

She couldn't.

"My dear?" Father lifted his eyes and studied her closely. After a moment, he shook his head and motioned toward the chair beside him. "Sit."

She didn't have the heart or energy to deny him, so she complied.

"This is a grim life we have. We rarely get to see the bright side, because Death is all we cater to. Yet, there is *life*, Inessa. All around us." When she didn't answer, he reached for her arm and patted it. "You are a good woman, don't let your tasks tell you otherwise. Take a look at the deer." His gaze darted toward the tree line. "When there are too many, they become ill and starve. They need help controlling their numbers—"

"We are not deer," she rushed to say, straightening as she turned to look at him. "We are more than that. The care-takers of the land, put here by the Great Ones to oversee until we are called home."

"And is Death not doing as the Great Ones command?" Father prompted softly, but concern flashed in his blue eyes.

Once Inessa thought she knew the answer. Hadeon was only a servant of the Great Ones, cleansing the excess. Yet, now, she wasn't certain. Why would Hlíf bring in a lifebringer if that were true?

"I think you are wise enough to know that answer," he said when she didn't respond to him.

Inessa exhaled and closed her eyes. The image of every pyre she'd ever seen flashed through her mind. Each fire had been a life, each person with a story to tell, and loved ones left behind to mourn their passing. She knew what that was like, what it was to suffer. But even as she grieved for the souls that had departed, Inessa knew she had a job to do.

"But does it make it the right?" Questioning the gods was never a clever thing to do. But then again, what could be worse than Death dealt out so freely?

Father picked up his whittling again and started cutting away the wooden pieces once more, seemingly content with her silence.

"I never pry because I know the toll your tasks take on you, but I believe you should entertain the idea of inviting someone into your life." He shook his head and pursed his lips before continuing. "Living with me, here, so far from the village? It isn't right, and it isn't good for you."

Inessa scoffed. "What is good or right about harvesting souls?" She reached for a discarded piece of shaved wood and twisted it in her grasp. "I understand why Mama wanted to run from Hadeon... How could I ever celebrate life when in so many ways I *am* Death?"

But maybe that was the point.

Deathbringers weren't meant to live; they were only meant to exist and then subtract.

Eleven

Sickness bloomed in the village like mountain flowers in the spring, but surprisingly, Inessa hadn't reaped any more souls. It was likely due to Stellan and the mark. Embla hadn't passed on, had even recovered to nearly her normal self. So had the other gravely ill individuals of Svetl.

Perhaps there was a way out of reaping without it killing her, as it had her mother.

Inessa bent to collect the logs she'd split. The sun was going down and there was a particular bite in the air, nipping at the tip of her nose. With the look of the dark, heavy clouds, another storm was on the way. Thankfully, she'd made bread and stew earlier. That would warm her if she became too chilled.

She ducked inside her home and dropped the logs next to the hearth to dry, then plopped into the chair in front of the fire.

Inessa bent to pick up her nalbinding, needing to make another pair of socks for herself. She looped the bone needle through the wool yarn, letting the repetition soothe her. For once, she didn't want to dwell on any thoughts surrounding Death.

It was curious though, how her thoughts drifted toward Stellan.

Jarl Kveld's son...with eyes so blue, so open and inviting.

Inessa wasn't one to blush or stumble over a man. She had never done such a thing in her youth, but Stellan was the sort of beautiful that a younger version of herself may have blushed in front of.

Perhaps if she had lived a different life, one not of a deathbringer, they would have met under different circumstances. Maybe she wouldn't have been as cynical in that life, more open to the idea of mingling with someone from Runestadt.

What would it be like, she wondered, to live a normal life? To taste his lips, and drink honey mead without much of a care?

The door opened, stirring Inessa from her thoughts. She turned to look, assuming it was her father.

"It's starting to snow already," Father said, dusting off his fur coat. He made his way toward the hearth, where he hung his cap and fur.

"Damn," Inessa muttered, too quietly for her father to hear. "Suppose we couldn't be so lucky to go without it for long." She swallowed roughly, tucking a piece of hair behind her ear. Her skin was warm to the touch, and she wondered if a girlish blush colored her cheeks or if it was that same cozy, comfortable sensation that Stellan had passed onto her hand the last time they met.

"Just came from Dagne's—"

"Oh?" Inessa leaned forward to study her father's expression and grinned when he waved her away. "I think it's sweet. I also know that Mama would have preferred you to find another."

He sighed. "I know. It's just..."

"Father, honestly, it's time." Inessa stood, depositing her nalbinding on the chair. She walked toward her father to embrace him. "You talk all the time of life. Well, what about you?" He remained quiet, so she continued. "I'll find somewhere else to live. Perhaps I'll even settle for someone like Einar."

The thought made her chuckle, which made her father laugh too. Einar wasn't a poor choice, but she only had platonic feelings for him. Sadly, that was how she felt when it came to the entire village, but she supposed that was why the surrounding villages communed once a year.

"Einar isn't such a bad pick, is he now?"

"Not my choice though," she huffed.

Of course Inessa had kissed a boy or two, but she'd never done anything more. She didn't want to bring a life into a world full of misery and pain, one that she knew all too well.

If she could end the cycle, so be it.

"All right, my girl. I had supper at Dagne's, it's been a long day of hard chores. I'm off to bed, and hopefully, you are too." He eyed the door, as if wondering if Hadeon would summon her in a few hours.

She wondered too.

Inessa hoped not.

"Good night, Father." She grinned a little as he turned and walked away. Once he was gone, she lit the candles on the table, then sat back down to work on her nalbinding until her eyes grew heavy.

Wake up!

Inessa swore, none too quietly, as she rose from the chair. Her eyes darted toward the table and judging by how the candles were now stubs, she'd been asleep for a few hours.

We need to go and quickly. His voice rolled around in her mind, rushed and panicked.

He was never usually in a hurry, but the last time they'd been in Stellan's presence, Hadeon had been out of sorts.

Inessa pressed her lips together and grabbed her fur coat, wrapping it around herself.

Move faster. His tone deepened, full of compulsion and Inessa had no option but to hurry out the door.

Nearly half a foot of snow had fallen since she'd been outside and it came down in such a heavy flurry, she could scarcely see Hadeon. She gritted her teeth as her legs moved of their own accord, bringing her closer to him.

Finally, Inessa's hand met his withers. She grabbed a fistful of his mane, then launched herself onto his back. Just barely on, he bolted into a canter, almost unseating her. He was still out of sorts and that meant Stellan was rankling him. Although she shouldn't be amused, it meant life stood a chance.

Inessa may have been a reaper, but that didn't mean she opposed life. She smiled a little.

Her glee didn't last long, not as the snow pelted her in the face and stung her eyes.

Hadeon veered from thei desolate path and brought them through the center of the village.

Smoke from the blazing hearths filled the air, but it didn't chase away the bite, nor cast away the snowflakes. She cringed as they plodded through the snow, but as Hadeon edged closer to the jarl's lodging, Inessa held her breath.

"No," she wheezed. "He's not even ill. None of them are.

Hadeon, we cannot do this!" Whether it was the jarl or his family, it didn't matter, she couldn't...

Yet, she had to. Even as she tried to slip from his back, her body refused.

Hadeon trotted toward the jarl's longhouse and the moon seemed to highlight the structure all the more. *Great Ones, why have you forsaken us all? Why let Death run rampant?* She clenched her teeth, quietly sobbing as she yearned to leap from Hadeon's back.

Be quick, Hadeon commanded.

In her years of reaping, she'd never taken a soul that wasn't ready. She knew the jarl wasn't ill, knew that his family was in perfect health. So, did this mean Hadean was taking a healthy soul before it was ready—murdering them?

At once, her body jerked, and she awkwardly landed in the snow. Through the haze of Hadeon's demands, she wondered if calling out to Stellan with her mind would do anything—could he hear her? Could he feel Death looming even from his village?

She scanned the area, her senses heightening as she stepped closer to the home. If she could fight it...

One step closer and her hand rose to push the door open. The fire emitted a warm glow, and as her eyes adjusted to the dimness inside, she felt a familiar pulse. A soul called to her, tethering her in place until Hadeon's will was done. They were ready and if Inessa didn't claim them, she'd prolong their life, keeping them from the Great Hall.

Inessa chewed her bottom lip, warring with what was right. Would this soul have been ready if it hadn't been for Hadeon's intervention? Would it have naturally grown tired of this world and longed for the heavens?

She grudgingly walked toward the adjacent room.

"Stop," Stellan's voice startled her.

She whirled around, her gaze darting toward the shadows. It wasn't long before she spotted him. Stellan stood just outside the light put off by the fire. She had hoped he'd be here, hoped he would come to stop her, but she hadn't anticipated how his presence felt like a beacon of hope amidst the darkness.

Yet there was tension in his stance, a conflict etched into his features.

"I told you the last time we saw one another that I'd have no choice but to fight you." His ethereal sword formed in his grasp, the golden glow encompassing his hand. "I'm sorry, Inessa." Sincerity coated his tone and glimmered in his eyes, along with a firm resolve.

As Inessa neared Stellan, he stepped into the light, his eyes locking onto hers.

"Stellan," she said softly, her voice carrying a mixture of urgency and sorrow.

You will not interrupt us this time. If she will not obey me...

Stellan's brows furrowed and he looked toward the door. A cold wind blew in, carrying snow with it. The strong gust snuffed out the fire and then Inessa clutched at her heart, falling to her knees.

You give me no choice. We must fight him together.

Inessa's hand jerked forward of its own accord, and she stared down at it, willing it to lower. *This is different.* Panic rose within her, tightening her throat. "No," she forced out. Yet, her body wouldn't obey, as if her consciousness had been shoved aside. Hadeon had taken over her being.

Stellan cursed under his breath. "Outside. Not in here. Even glamoured we'll rouse them." He backed away, cross-stepping until he stood outside.

Before she could respond, Hadeon pushed her forward, and she lunged at Stellan. Her arms lifted, sword already in her grasp. With the downward arc, her blade met Stellan's.

If you will not obey, I will do it. He cannot hear me, and you cannot speak. Hadeon's voice growled in her mind.

The clashing of their swords reverberated through her forearms, into her very marrow. Inessa moved with precision, matching Stellan blow for blow. She dodged as he brought his sword low, nearly striking her. He seemed to hold back a fraction, as if he didn't want to harm her.

She believed that.

Except what choice did he have when she seemingly pushed him further and further. If only she could scream...

Inessa tried, but nothing more than a grunt came out. Hadeon set a punishing pace for them—slashing, diving, driving forward with the blade. But Stellan was a jarl's son, expected to train as a warrior. He was a solid fighter. And if she could be possessed, so could he.

In a swift motion, Stellan feigned a strike, catching Inessa off guard. He tripped her, and because the snow was too high, she lost her balance and fell to the ground. Her face collided with the snowpack, and the cold sucked her breath away.

Quickly, she spun around, but Stellan pinned her before she could climb to her feet. His golden brows furrowed in question and Inessa wondered what he saw written on her face. A plea? Hadeon's anger? Her lust?

Get him off of us! Hadeon roared.

"Inessa, please," Stellan said hoarsely, his breath coming in ragged draws. "I don't want to fight you."

And she didn't either. She wanted to flee from Hadeon's tainted grasp. Yet he had her very life in his proverbial grasp.

"H-h-help," she stammered, eyes widening as her hand flexed and the idea of grabbing the knife in her boot resounded in her mind.

"Get up. Take the knife."

Something clicked at that moment. What if this was how the last lifebringer died? What if Hadeon had grown more hungry for souls, more demanding, and forced his vessel to claim life?

Stellan didn't let off her, but his eyes studied her face. Then he looked around, perhaps noticing the lack of a horse. He swore none too quietly. "Forgive me," he said before he leaned forward, pressing his lips to hers in a searing kiss.

She'd been kissed before, but none were like this.

Just like when he'd touched her hand, Stellan's lips warmed every inch of her body, chasing away the chill, the shadows, and the despair that seemed ever present. His lips manipulated hers, slowly, urgently, demanding something from her.

Fire spread through her, lighting the inky tendrils of Hadeon's control ablaze and disintegrating them.

Inessa gasped as Death's control eased.

Stellan's grip loosened, and she relinquished her hold on the sword. It dawned on her that she had regained control of her body.

Inessa, no! Hadeon's voice was a distant thing as Stellan's warmth surged into her.

Then, all too quickly, Stellan withdrew and rocked back on his heels. He jerked his head to the side and snarled at the prancing horse. "I could have killed her!" His face, which had nearly looked serene moments ago, contorted with such rage that Inessa scrambled backward.

Stellan glanced her way, then back at Hadeon. "Hlíf will come for you."

To that, Hadeon only snorted. He looked to Inessa, then he bolted for the woods.

Inessa felt the tension slip from her. "Thank you," she murmured. "I didn't want—"

"I can't believe he did that." Stellan sounded so incredulous. "He would use you as a shield."

His surprise caught her off guard. She touched her lips and glanced in the direction Hadeon had gone. "I think...I think I know what happened to the last lifebringer."

Color rushed to his cheeks. Inessa surmised it wasn't from embarrassment, but rather rage. Understanding filtered into his gaze, and he swore under his breath. "Will you come with me?" His voice was so quiet.

After what he'd done, she couldn't say no. Inessa took a deep breath, closing her eyes for a brief second. She nodded.

Stellan's face lit up with relief, and he quickly helped her to her feet. He turned and walked toward the opposite path of which she'd come, and there, standing hitched to a tree was a shaggy palomino horse that reminded Inessa very much of its rider.

When he reached his horse, he turned to Inessa and helped her up, then followed behind her. His body pressed against her, and his warmth washed over her like the sun in the summer.

Heat filled Inessa's cheeks. For when the night air licked at her skin, she felt the contrast of the cold against her burning skin.

"Th-thank you." Inessa's voice sounded frail even to her. She hated herself for it.

"You don't have to thank me," Stellan said, his breath tickling the nape of her neck.

She felt him withdraw a fraction, then his horse took off into a steady run. And for the first time that she could recall, she didn't look over her shoulder, wondering where Hadeon was, or if he was watching her.

Somewhere along the way, she'd fallen asleep, because when she roused, Stellan's arms were around her, securing her against his chest.

The horse had halted, for how long Inessa didn't know. Judging by the lazy leg it cocked in the rear, it had been a few moments at least.

She sat up and turned to glance at Stellan. "Sorry." Confused as to where they were, she looked around, expecting to find the lake, the village, something familiar but no. Before her was a wooden home, not built in the style of Svetl but that of Runestadt.

He must have seen the question, felt the way she stiffened —perhaps knew she was readying to fight, because Stellan sighed. "This is my home." He glanced at the structure. Wooden beams jutted from the roofline like horns, and the shakes on the roof gave it a scale-like appearance. "I thought perhaps you'd want a little more reprieve from Hadeon— from whatever he has in store for you." He clicked his tongue and shook his head. "I cannot protect you if you're away from me."

"Protect me?" Inessa asked in a strangled voice. "There is no protecting me." She thought of her mother, of how she'd wanted to stop *this* way of living.

Stellan snorted. "Do you really believe that?" he asked softly. "Come inside, have a bit to eat, warm up, and I'll take you back home."

"After tonight?" Hadeon would protect his cause and in doing so, would end her life if she got in the way. There was another reaper waiting to be made out there, and he could wake them in a blink.

She refocused on Stellan, who'd already returned from putting his horse away. He cocked his head and motioned toward his home. Hopeful.

What had she to lose?

Twelve

s soon as Inessa stepped over the threshold, the scent of simmering stew met her. Her stomach grumbled and she brushed her hand against her abdomen.

A table sat before the hearth, fairly new since the wood still had a sheen to it and lacked the scarring of time and use. Inessa surveyed the open room, catching the hunting gear on the far side of where she stood. Fur rugs had been laid out on the dirt floor and walls too.

A door next to the hearth made her wonder about another room, and how big it was considering the spaciousness of the living area. Stellan's home was easily three times the size of hers.

"Are you going to stand rigidly the entire time, or are you going to sit?" Stellan walked toward the long table. He used his foot to pull out a chair, then motioned to it. "I'm not going to bite." He moved around the room, lighting candles as he went.

Inessa folded her arms and shook her head. Maybe not

bite, but kiss? She bit her bottom lip, chastising herself for even thinking of it again.

Stellan grabbed a bowl and filled it with stew, then set it onto the table. "Warm yourself." He slid the bowl toward her, then served himself too.

Unable to deny herself, she sat and scooted forward. She grabbed the bowl and brought it to her mouth, then drank the broth greedily.

After a few mouthfuls of the briny stock, she set the bowl down and watched as Stellan grabbed a loaf of bread and plopped it between them.

"Am I mad for thinking Hadeon killed Hlíf's last lifebringer?" she finally asked, her voice barely above a whisper.

Stellan sat and inched his chair closer to hers. She was certain that if he moved his knee it would brush against hers. His expression grew earnest. "No, but then again I don't know you or Hadeon well." He sighed, shaking his head. "I could've hurt you, because of him..." He dragged his hand down his face. "Hlíf told me of their history..."

Did it differ from what Inessa knew? She knew Hadeon and Hlíf didn't see eye to eye, but generally they got along. They were two sides of the same scale.

Inessa clenched her teeth and nodded. "What he did back there... He has never done that before." She stared at the flickering flame of the candle. "What did Hlíf tell you?"

"A lot," he said with a half-hearted chuckle. "I haven't slept much since she woke me, because we've been trying to put out the soul fires, if you will." Stellan tore a chunk of bread from the loaf and ate it. "She told me of the never ending cycle between life and death. We know this, and there is a balance—you know this. But when Death—Hadeon—

grows restless and greedy, he attempts to tip the scales. Think of it as a weather pattern, I suppose." He shrugged and Inessa couldn't blame him. He appeared confused.

She would have been too, had it only been three days since her awakening. However, Hlíf seemed to be an enlightening mistress. One that shed light on the knowledge Stellan needed. Whereas, Hadeon had given her scraps over the years and kept many secrets.

"But why?" she sounded weak, even to herself. And she hated how she didn't have answers.

"It is his nature, being one of darkness. He isn't evil, as we believe, but driven by his shadows and need for souls; they empower him. But it's never enough. So when he is overcome by gluttony, Hlíf begins this cycle. It has been so since the dawn of all things."

She chewed her bottom lip, weighing his words. Finally an answer, one she supposed she'd gathered throughout the years. She had hoped it had been more than gluttony, that Hadeon was simply an evil spirit that must be conquered.

No, Hadeon was just a greedy spirit.

Inessa watched Stellan carefully, waiting for him to continue. She reached across the table for a drink, throat dry from her growing nerves.

"If Hadeon continues and the scale bottoms out...the other gods will awaken."

Hlíf and Hadeon were separate entities from the gods. Spirits, or minor dieties, however one wanted to look at them. They were of the earthly realm and not of the heavens, created to exist on this plain, and be tended to by the gods, should they step out of line.

She paused her reach halfway to the bowl and dropped her hand. "They haven't been awake for—"

"Nearly five hundred sixty years," he finished.

Her throat squeezed shut as she tried to dismiss earlier events. Not because she didn't see the truth, but because she *did*.

Hadeon was claiming too many souls, too fast, creating discord, and Hlíf was fighting back. In doing so, they'd surely garner the attention of the gods, wake them from their slumber, and they'd hurl whatever punishment they saw fit down on the earth to keep the two of them in check.

Waking the gods wouldn't benefit Hadeon, not really. But he wanted the souls for himself, wanted the rush of power. Inessa had seen this herself, the heady rush in his gaze when she'd exit a home after reaping.

No, if the gods awakened, it would benefit neither him nor Hlíf—and especially not earth.

Inessa glanced out the window. Inessa glanced out the window. Moonlight spilled over the landscape. A flash of gold caught Inessa's eye. She blinked, wondering what it was, then dismissed her initial thought. It couldn't be a pair of eyes, watching them. No, she was safe here in Stellan's home and her body hummed with that truth.

"If Hadeon decided I was no longer of service to him, he'd take my soul. Long ago, reapers and bringers weren't needed. But the last time they rivaled, there was a cleanse. Hadeon and Hlíf were punished by the gods, they could no longer use their powers without a vessel. And so, that is why we exist."

"To serve as their consciences." Stellan made a noise of surprise.

"What would become of us if the gods awakened this time?"

She shrugged. "I don't know. And I don't want to know either."

Inessa scooped up some stew with the bread. "So, we fight back, because what else do we have to lose?" The last lifebringer had fought back, left a bread crumb for them to see in a way. So maybe that was the solution. Stellan scooted his chair closer to hers. "I will do whatever I can to help. Hlíf is readying to join the fight. She already interferes, as you experienced." He grabbed her hands, squeezed them and dropped his gaze to her lips.

She felt the heat of his stare and recalled the feeling of his kiss, his searing touch. Inessa brought her fingers to his lips and brushed over them. "Was that Hlíf, or you when you kissed me?" Why did she want it to be *him*?

His bright blue eyes caught hers and he smiled warmly. "Both. I didn't know I could do that. Not until I felt life screaming from the inside, as if I were about to burst. I wanted him out of you, and I...just acted." He pursed his lips for a moment. "I didn't mean—"

"To what, save me?" Inessa quirked a brow and shook her head. "Look at us both. Vessels to be used and abused however our entities deem fit."

Stellan squeezed her hand again, and she didn't bother to pull away. His broad palm covered her fingers with ease. "You have a choice in this, you know. You're a fighter. I've seen that myself. Don't let Hadeon write your destiny for you."

His words resonated deep within her, stirring something she had tried to bury—hope. Still, fear and doubt mingled together, making it difficult to find the will to fight. She looked at Stellan, seeing the determination in his eyes, and felt a spark ignite within her.

Her brows furrowed. "I'm human. How on earth can I

cut my own path when we're talking about beings as old as the Great Ones?" She studied his face, saw his brow crease.

He went quiet and stared at her.

Inessa closed the distance between them and brushed her lips against his, tentatively at first but when he didn't pull away, she increased the pressure.

Stellan wrapped his arms around her waist loosely, as if he were waiting for her to pull back, but Inessa craved more of his warmth. She wanted him to chase away the chill buried in her bones.

His fingers slid her fur coat off and it pooled around her. He dragged his gaze to hers, and a silent question—*Are you certain?*—floated between them.

She nodded a fraction and allowed him to undress her entirely. Inessa thought she'd feel the bite of the cooler air, but his hands breathed fire beneath her skin. "We can talk after, since that's why I'm here," she murmured as his lips trailed down her chin, to her neck and his coarse beard tickled her throat.

Stellan chuckled, lifting his head to look up at her. "After, we can devise a plan for you." He lifted his hand, stroking a strand of hair away from her face. "But now, I'm going to listen to what you want from me, and you can take what you need, Inessa."

And for the first time in a long time, she felt free and ready to fight for her freedom, no matter what it took.

INESSA WOKE AS THE FIRST RAYS OF LIGHT FILTERED through the window, casting a soft glow in the room. She blinked, glancing around to remind herself where she was—who she was with.

Stellan's breath washed over the back of her neck and for a beat, she allowed herself to savor the comfort he provided.

The steady cadence of his breath nearly lulled her back to sleep.

In. Out. In. Out.

Despite wanting to focus on the steady rhythm of his breathing, her tumultuous thoughts returned. She carefully and slowly turned to face him. He rolled to his back, as if waiting for her to nestle onto his chest.

Inessa hadn't last night and didn't know if it was expected of her now. In all her years, she'd never been moved to sleep with a man, but there was a stillness in Stellan that she yearned for. He chased the cold from her bones and quieted the voices in her mind.

He hadn't taken anything more than she was willing to give and when their bodies entwined in a desperate bid for connection, he hadn't rushed a moment.

But now, as dawn broke, reality reasserted itself, and Inessa knew they had to face the challenges ahead.

Carefully, she extricated herself from Stellan's bed and sat up, wrapping her arms around her knees. The air was cool, and she shivered slightly, the chill seeping into her skin. She stared out the window, spying new mounds of snow.

Movement at the edge of the wood caught Inessa's attention. The Great Wolf, Hlíf, stood there and nodded, as if beckoning Inessa. The early morning light clung to her ivory pelt, causing her to nearly glow with the goodness that must have encapsulate her being. Her wise eyes, rather than deep and haunting, were full of everything she represented: life.

The wolf turned back toward the woods, but Inessa knew she was meant to follow.

Inessa dressed quickly and headed out the door, racing toward the wood line.

A soft rustling of leaves followed by the sound of footsteps, and then out of the shadows emerged a massive wolf, her fur as white as freshly fallen snow and her eyes a piercing yellow. Hlíf moved with a grace and power that spoke of ancient wisdom and strength.

Inessa's breath caught as she stepped up to the beast, impressed by her size, and comforted by her calming demeanor. There was an unspoken gentleness about her.

Wise eyes homed in on Inessa. "Hello, Inessa," she rumbled in greeting.

"What am I supposed to do?" Inessa blurted as all her thoughts collided and came out in a sharp question.

"I will help you as much as I can, but Stellan is my vessel. And though Dcath is not my realm, should you threaten him, he will do what is necessary."

She understood. Hadeon would do the same.

"However, you know that as vessels, you don't have the same weaknesses Hadeon and I share. Our touches are like fire and ice to one another and weaken us. You and Stellan can touch one another without being weakened. That is not to say destruction by mortal means isn't effective."

"Is that what happened to the last lifebringer?" She narrowed her eyes and looked up at Hlíf, waiting for the truth.

The wolf's gaze flicked over Inessa's shoulder. Footsteps fell in the snow and Inessa spun to see Stellan approaching.

Sunlight bathed his face, rays catching on the find blond

hairs of his beard. Stellan approached the wolf, extended his hand and brushed down her nose tenderly.

Gods, he was beautiful.

Inessa turned her attention back to the wolf and Hlíf continued on.

"The last lifebringer was slain by the reaper. A similar situation had been brewing, and Hadeon possessed the reaper. Except, he feared at that moment that if he continued it would awaken the gods."

The wolf continued. "He cannot help what he is. He is greedy and sometimes, he needs to be reminded of that. When Hadeon loses a grasp on souls, when the wrath of the gods comes down upon the mortals..."

Hopelessness swirled inside of Inessa. This didn't sound like anything they could permanently fix—it was a cycle. "Can you stop him?"

Hlíf closed her eyes for a moment and shook her head ruefully. "I can delay him. I could fight him even, but if he is bent on collecting souls that are not due to him yet, there's not much I can do. If we war for long, we risk the attention of the Great Ones." Hlíf regarded them both with a piercing gaze.

"Doesn't upsetting the balance, threatening to unleash chaos, isn't that enough to garner the attention of the Great Ones?" Inessa tried to lessen the bite in her words, but she was thoroughly done with how the Great Ones seemed to manipulate all of them.

The wolf chuffed a small laugh and relaxed on her haunches. "He would need to decimate a grand portion of the continent, which he seems as though he's on the path to do." She sighed, glancing up toward the sky.

Inessa's brow furrowed. Damn the gods. The useless lot.

"It has happened a few times over the eons." Hlíf sighed, her head lowering a fraction. "When the Great Ones touch on the mortal plain, all seems well to begin with. This is during their assessment, and there is no Death, only Life. The scales fill until the breaking point—and that is when judgment falls on the mortals. In order to truly balance the scales out once again, they destroy the land. By fire, by quake, by flood."

Inessa gasped, her knees nearly giving out. "What?" The Great Ones were beings of immense power, ancient forces that maintained the delicate balance of the world. But they'd level the land, destroying nearly all life just because Death became greedy? How did that achieve anything different?

"They do this, because if neither Life nor Death can be balanced, mankind suffers the punishment. If they start from scratch, begin again—"

"No," Inessa hissed.

The Great Ones intervention was something to be feared.

And it was not something that Inessa could allow to happen.

Stellan shifted and leaned against a tree, folding his arms. "Is there no other way? Can we not find a way to weaken Hadeon's influence without direct confrontation?"

The Great Wolf pondered for a moment. "There may be a way. Undermine his power, weaken the foundation upon which he stands. His strength comes from Death, and we are in his season—winter. We cannot control the seasons, but the Great Ones can, yet we don't want them involved." Hlíf paused and cocked her head. "If there was a way that I could touch him until he fell into a great slumber, allow the scales to even out without life furthering the imbalance... You have a spot of hope to shift the scales to a safe place."

"But that won't change his way of thinking. We'll end up here once again." Annoyance rippled through Inessa. They needed a solution altogether. If they didn't have one, there was no point.

She gritted her teeth and looked at the village streets. No one had opened their doors yet, no windows creaked open, yet the sun washed the land in light.

Stellan glanced at Inessa, a flicker of hope in his eyes. "You're right. What if we can trap him for a time, show him that this will only lead to the destruction of mankind?"

Perhaps it was because Inessa had grown up with Death, had only ever seen the cruelties life had to offer, but she wasn't contemplating gently convincing Hadeon. She knew he wouldn't listen to gentleness. He'd scoff at her, call her weak, and kill her.

Inessa chewed on the side of her thumb. "What does Hadeon hold most dear? What does he fear?"

Hlíf's eyes zeroed in on Inessa. "He fears me. Fears insignificance too."

Inessa loosed a frustrated breath and paced away from them, only to turn on her heel and approach again, reconsidering their plan. "If subdued, perhaps we can make him see the sense, that if he should continue, he'll be without lives to reap and the wrath of the Great Ones will rain down on the both of you."

"So, if we stage an attack on Hadeon, subdue him enough to reason with, then perhaps this will end?"

Not once and for all, because even Hlíf confirmed it had happened repeatedly over the eons of time, but it would perhaps settle the precarious situation they found themselves in until next time. Perhaps then the next reaper and lifebringer would be wiser than she and Stellan, knowing how to avoid such conflicts.

Hlíf nodded her head. "I can do that. I can wound him, and that will sap away his energies so you two can move in."

Stellan nodded. "Tonight then?"

"Tonight," Hlíf said and stood on all fours. "We will find you, Inessa, before you're able to claim a soul. But we will not alert you, other than this warning." She crossed the distance between them, brushed her warm muzzle against Inessa's side and offered what Inessa considered to be a smile.

The wolf spun on her haunches and leaped into the cover of the bushes. One moment she was there and in the next, gone.

Something akin to hope blossomed in Inessa's chest, or maybe it was purpose. She and Stellan had a plan, a way to fight Hadeon without resorting to a conflict that would incite the wrath of the Great Ones. They would weaken his control, inspire hope, and slowly tip the scales back toward balance.

Thirteen

⤜∽⤛

"I suppose this is where we part ways," Inessa said as she turned to face Stellan.

His warm gaze didn't waver from hers. "First, I want to show you how much of a stake I have in this. And that, no matter what, I will fight." Stellan closed the distance between them. He brushed his knuckles against the curve of her jaw and pressed his forehead to hers. "When this is done, I don't want you to think that we are." Stellan's warm breath washed over her cool cheek. "We are only beginning, you and I. And if you'll have me, Inessa, I want to continue to learn more about you."

"We will see where the road leads us. Now...what did you want to show me?"

He brushed past her and stepped free of the woods, toward the village once again.

"Where are we heading?" Inessa walked by his side as he strode through the snow drifts.

"Just a house down the way." He didn't look down at her, but kept his eyes trained on the house not far from where they were. It was built in the same style as Stellan's, but on the roof, instead of beams that looked like antlers, a carved dragon's head had been carved. In the early dawn light, it looked like an evil spirit and Inessa grimaced.

Stellan continued forward toward the façade of the house, and Inessa reached for his hand.

"We are not glamoured. We will be seen!" she said.

"Trust me," he said before continuing inside.

Inessa scanned the new surroundings, a habit she'd picked up from reaping and entering so many strange homes. She needed to know escape routes, needed to know where she could quickly run or hide.

The inside was a near replica of what Stellan's home looked like, except there were more furs lining the wall, and wooden shelves held bowls, cups and the like.

Stellan motioned for her to follow, so she did. He led her to a doorway where a small girl, likely the age of ten, slumbered.

Even in the soft light of the morning, Inessa could see the sweat gleaming on the girl's brow. The grayness of her complexion and how dull her blond hair, which Inessa assumed would look like Stellan's had she been of good health, spoke of illness.

It wasn't fair. None of this was.

Inessa angled herself so that she could better see into the room, then drew in a sharp breath as she spotted a familiar face—Jarl Kveld. At the same instant, he looked up at them, his eyes weary with worry and exhaustion.

Her hair...the jarl... The girl in the bed was Stellan's sister! Guilt washed over Inessa as she realized the personal stakes Stellan had in this fight. She stepped closer, her gaze softening as she took in the girl's pale face.

"I'm sorry," she blurted before she turned on her heel and ran from the room. Inessa didn't bother stopping until she stood outside.

Greedily, she sucked in the cold air and tried to calm her pounding heart.

Footsteps shuffled behind her, and she knew without looking they were Stellan's. She'd grown accustomed to his presence already.

"Why didn't you tell me sooner?" she whispered harshly and turned to face him.

He sighed, his shoulders sagging slightly. "Because my family isn't the only one that is suffering. I couldn't stomach using Nilia against you." Stellan dragged his hand down his chin, frowning.

It was the first time Inessa had seen him so drawn looking, and his typical glow seemed to fade.

"But she needs help, Inessa. And we need to stop Hadeon before more people suffer like this. I've done what I can for her, but it is up to her soul to fight. If she loses the battle..." He swallowed roughly.

Inessa couldn't do anything for Nilia. Her touch was a Death sentence; it was Stellan's touch that would gift life.

Inessa would be seeing Nilia again—very soon.

"Your whole village is like this?" The last time she had been in the village it hadn't been this severe, and none were quite ready to be reaped, so she had no way of knowing.

"Very nearly. Some have bounced back."

The gravity of his words hung in the air. Inessa raked her hands through her mussed hair and loosed a shaky breath. "Show me."

And so he did.

There was so much sickness in Runestadt, far more than Svetl. At this rate, it would spread to the continent.

Inessa pressed her fingers to her temples. "Tonight cannot come soon enough." Runestadt would take the better part of the day to venture through, and it would nearly be dusk when she arrived back at home. "I need to head back. Can you take me there?"

Stellan nodded. "Of course."

THE SUN HAD SET AND ONLY THE FAINTEST DREGS of light touched the snow-covered ground by the time Stellan arrived in Svetl. He halted his horse, which allowed for Inessa to dismount. The illness that had swept through her village left it eerily silent. Usually there was some sort of joyous laughter or singing, but there was nothing.

"Tonight," he said, then added, "I will see you soon." He yanked the reigns, and was off, back down the trail that led to his home.

Inessa still had a small trek before she made it to her house. As her boots crunched the icy turf, her mind strayed to the truth— a reaper had slain a lifebringer. Well, *that* wouldn't be happening again, not if she could help it.

She worried on her bottom lip, losing herself to her tumultuous thoughts. Before she knew it, she stood in front of her home. Her father emerged, his eyes wide. "Inessa?" Relief flooded his face as he walked forward, and surprisingly, Einar was on his heels.

"So, you're alive after all?" Einar grinned at her. She knew that if she were closer to him, he'd take to tussling her hair, like she was a child.

Inessa managed a weak smile, fatigue weighing heavily on her shoulders. She nodded at her father and friend, grateful for their concern despite Einar's teasing tone. "I'm alive," she confirmed, her voice hoarse from her journey. "But I could really use a hot meal right about now."

"A bath wouldn't hurt either." Einar wrinkled his nose, mocking her again.

"Don't mind him. He's brought some good news and is in one of his famous moods." By that, Father meant Einar was into his cups and loud.

At least Einar wasn't mean when he drank.

Her father ushered her inside their humble home, where a fire crackled in the hearth and the smell of roasted venison wafted from the table. Inessa sank into a wooden chair at the table, letting out a content sigh as warmth enveloped her cold body.

Einar settled into the seat opposite her, his gaze intense as he observed her every move. They'd been friends for far too long and she wondered if he knew, if he could tell she'd been with someone? Did it even matter? No, it didn't.

Deciding not to call more attention to herself, she simply stared down at the bowl her father slid in front of her.

"I've got news. The illness seems to be easing up. My mother was beginning to show signs of catching it just a few days ago. A bad cough and fever, but she's bounced back now." Inessa glanced up at him just as Einar smiled broadly. "You know how she is, tough as old leather."

At this, she smiled too. Inessa would have to ask Stellan if that had been his doing. She assumed he'd touched those who were beginning to fall ill as well as those who were nearing their end.

A cure to the Death spread.

"I'm glad to hear that. I wish her well."

Einar's smile only grew. "Thank you."

The warmth of the hearth and the aroma of the stew worked their magic on Inessa, reviving her spirits as she listened to Einar's report about the illness slowly easing its grip on the village. She couldn't help but feel a swell of gratitude toward Stellan.

"Is that all you came by for then?" Inessa finally asked.

His brows shot up, and he grinned broadly. "Maybe I came to annoy you, eh?"

Her father shook his head. "No, he came because I saw him earlier and had been wondering where you were. Thought you might be together."

Inessa couldn't help but curl her lip at the insinuation. *Not him, Father.* And despite her friendship with Einar, she was itching for him to leave so she could speak with her father alone.

His eyes lingered on her for a moment, and she lifted a brow. Einar was too focused on stuffing bread into his mouth to catch it, but her father seemed to pick up on the cue.

Once her friend had finished eating, he stood and patted his thighs. "Well, I should be on my way. Ren is watching my mother." She was the girl that lived next door, a slip of a thing with wide blue eyes.

"Safe travels, Einar. And may the Great Ones be with your mother," Inessa said as she stood, but mentioning the gods who sat back watching the destruction of their people, and would only act to raze the world, made her mouth dry.

Her father slowly, too damn slowly, ushered Einar out of the house, and once he said his goodbyes pinned Inessa with a questioning glance.

"I was in Runestadt," she murmured and stood only so she could pace the floor. "The jarl's son—"

"Stellan?" His brows furrowed.

Right. I haven't told him yet.

"He's the lifebringer," she said.

Realization dawned on him, and he nodded, motioning for her to continue.

"I'll keep the story brief, not that it matters." Inessa bit the inside of her cheek as she thought of the night spent in Stellan's arms. "Hadeon," she whispered his name, afraid he'd bolt toward the door, "is attempting to upset the balance. Should I continue to reap for him, Hlíf will stand against him, then the Great Ones would take notice, raze the world." She sounded mad even to her ears, but her father seemed to take it all in stride.

His lips twitched, not in a smile, but frustration. As if he'd heard something similar before.

"I'm not backing down, Father. I refuse to stand by and do his dark deeds, pushing our people ever closer to destruction. Tonight, when Hadeon comes for me because he is driven to collect these poor damned souls, I will fight back. Please, don't try to stop me, and whatever you do, don't get in the way."

"So I stand to lose you too?" He shook his head and closed the distance between them, his hands on her shoulders. "What sort of father would I be if I stood by idly as you fought?"

"The kind that lives." Tears welled in her eyes, and she looked toward the ceiling to stop them. "Please don't," she whispered.

"My girl," her father said and cupped her cheek. "I must.

I couldn't bear to live with myself if I stood by and did nothing while you..."

She couldn't blame him. He'd lost his wife, and he would likely lose his daughter. At least concerning the latter, he stood a chance at changing the outcome. Inessa wouldn't let him, yet still, she withdrew from him and nodded her consent. "Very well. Before I leave tonight, Stellan will be waiting with Hlíf, and she will attack Hadeon enough to weaken him. They cannot fight for long, or they risk drawing the Great Ones' attention."

"I'll do all that I can to help." Her father leaned forward and brushed a kiss against her forehead.

"Just...be careful," she whispered and wrapped her arms around him in a tight embrace. "I'm not ready to lose you either."

Fourteen

Inessa didn't dare venture to the barn, to see if Hadeon lurked within. If he wanted her, he'd not hesitate to come calling. Despite having the chance to sleep, she couldn't seem to. For every time she closed her eyes, the anticipation of Hadeon's demands claimed her.

The floorboards outside her bedroom creaked, and she sat up. Her father appeared in her doorway with a lantern. The warm glow bathed his weathered face, and he sighed. "Just checking to see if you were still here."

Guilt gnawed at her. He knew her too well. She would bolt away from here if it meant sparing him. "I'm surprised too."

The barn door slammed, and Inessa jumped from her bed to peer out the window. "He's coming," she said, just as the silhouette of the horse emerged. His crimped mane billowed in the cool air, and his proud head bobbed as he strode toward the house.

Heart pounding, Inessa whirled around and grabbed at her clothes and began dressing.

"How will Stellan know to come?"

"Because he's already here." It wouldn't surprise her if Stellan had camped in the woods not far from her home.

Inessa pulled on her last layer of clothing and brushed past her father. He stopped her by placing a hand on her shoulder and glanced toward the door.

"Don't you think he'll be suspicious?"

She snorted. "Hadeon is so sure of himself. So confident that Death will overpower all, that he wouldn't stop and consider that I would try—or in the very least—succeed in stopping him."

He chuckled humorlessly. "That is for certain." With that, he let her go and followed outside. For a moment, he stared as Hadeon approached, and maybe that should have been the horse's first warning, but he ignored her father.

"Hadeon," Inessa drawled. "I know what you're doing, and it must stop. You know this ends with the Great Ones awakening, the same cycle as before. "

Foolish mortal. You cannot tell a Death god what they can and cannot do. Now, get on. His words held the compulsion that gave her no choice.

She gritted her teeth and stiffly walked toward him, trying her best to delay the inevitable.

With no sign of Stellan nearby or Hlíf, Inessa was forced to mount Hadeon. She grudgingly settled onto his back, then cast a glance toward her father. Hadeon spun and bolted down the pathway, but he didn't venture into the village, rather straight toward Runestadt.

She didn't want to think about Stellan in fear Hadeon would slip into her mind and divulge everything. But she did hope he was near and ready.

Trees flashed by them in a blur, and more than a few times Inessa had to duck out of the way of branches.

Without the moon above, she had to rely solely on his vision. And while her eyesight improved a fraction when it was time to reap, it was not like seeing during the day.

"Are you trying to kill me as well?" she griped and lowered herself so that she lay across his neck to dodge another low hanging limb.

Not yet.

She blinked, uncertain if that was a hint of humor, or if he truly planned on ending her life.

Inessa shuddered and remained quiet for the duration of the ride.

The gates to Runestadt greeted them with unlit torches and open doors. She surmised it was Stellan's doing, ushering them in.

"Why are we here?" she whispered.

Can't you smell it? That lingering moment before we sweep over the souls, it oozes from this place.

She inhaled sharply, and though she couldn't smell what he described, she could smell the sickness, a pungent sourness alongside the stench of rot.

Hadeon trotted forward, homing in on the jarl's lodgings. Except as he bolted forward, he crow-hopped to the side, unseating Inessa. She landed with a hard smack on the ground and winced as she stared in the direction Hadeon looked.

At first, Inessa's eyes were drawn toward Stellan. His broad frame seemed to glow, despite the lacking moon. He held his sword out, warding Hadeon off, but it was Hlíf who bounded forward and held Hadeon's focus.

The white wolf's form appeared as a ghostly blur against the darkened landscape. All Inessa could do was watch.

Hlíf approached, head held high. "Hadeon, I say this once and once only. Stop your reapings, and cease spreading illness across the land. Give the people a chance to heal, and then you may begin your antics again—"

"Never," Hadeon spoke defiantly and swirled his head. His mane covered his face, shrouding it much like a thick billow of smoke or ash. Inessa could feel the loathing emanating from him, and it caused her hair to raise on the back of her neck.

"I will warn you once more. Stand down, Hadeon," Hlíf said in a voice that was both gentle and firm.

Hadeon reared up, his hooves lashing the air before crashing down. He charged at Hlíf. The wolf, quicker to maneuver, danced around him as if this were nothing more than a game of chase.

Hlíf growled lowly. Standing next to Hadeon, she didn't look much smaller than him, and Inessa understood why he became frightened in her presence. She snarled, revealing her white fangs.

Hadeon didn't get a chance to respond again, for Hlíf leaped toward him with a speed that belied her size. Hadeon barely had time to react, bolting aside to avoid her attack.

Inessa felt helpless as she watched. She flexed her fingers, summoning her blade in case things escalated too quickly.

Something moved in the corner of her eye. She pivoted and saw Stellan approaching with his hands held out.

"It's time to bind Hadeon," he said as the two gods clashed with a force that sent shockwaves through the ground. Stellan jerked his head toward the commotion and

Inessa followed his line of sight. "And we have to do it quickly."

"How are *we* supposed to bind *him*?"

Stellan grimaced. "When Hlíf sinks her teeth into him, it'll weaken them both. I need to jump onto his back so I can push a surge of my power into him."

She nodded.

Hlíf lunged at Hadeon, her fangs scraping along his back leg. Hadeon stumbled, nearly falling over.

Stellan didn't spare another word and bolted for Hadeon's prone form. Inessa ran behind him, eyeing the limping Hlíf as she slid to the ground. As much as Inessa wanted to rush to her aid, she needed to make sure Stellan succeeded.

He climbed onto Hadeon, who was just gathering his wits enough to stabilize but still unsteady The pair of them fumbled forward. Yet Hadeon must have realized his passenger wasn't Inessa because he bucked wildly, trying his best to unseat Stellan. Hlíf's bite had drained him, and so the attempt to be rid of his rider failed.

Stellan ran his hands down Hadeon's shoulders, as the horse spun to shake him off. He lifted his hands and gripped Hadeon's neck.

"Inessa, my pack!" Stellan cried. "It's near Hlíf." He wound his hands through Hadeon's thick mane, trapping him. "There is rope."

Gritting her teeth, Inessa bolted toward Hlíf and spotted the leather sack. She slid on her knees and rummaged around until her fingers brushed the rough fiber. She jumped to her feet and ran for Hadeon, who spun around and drank her in with furious eyes.

You dare betray me? Hadeon's knees wobbled as Stellan drove his power into him.

Maybe there would have been a fraction of guilt about betraying him, if she didn't know that he had slain her mother, and aimed to kill hundreds of other innocents, while bringing the end of the world down on them all.

Hadeon collapsed to the ground, and Inessa quickly moved in. Stellan shifted off of his back but kept his hands on the horse's neck.

She wrapped the rope around Hadeon's legs, effectively hobbling him for the moment. Too weakened in this state to even thrash, Hadeon let out a heavy groan. "I dare to fight for life, Hadeon. How dare you speak of betrayal when I've served you all these years. And even still, when I know what you did to my mother." Inessa stood her ground, her voice steady. "This must stop, Hadeon. The killing, lording the promise of Death over me and my father."

You cannot defeat me!

Inessa growled in frustration. "It's not about defeating you, Hadeon. It's about stopping this madness. The Great Ones will come if you don't cease this. They'll bring destruction upon us all." And though she didn't quite know if her power would even work on him, she knelt before the horse and placed her palm against his forehead.

Closing her eyes, she pushed the knowledge Hlíf had shared, showing the Great Ones anger, their arrival and cleansing of the land, onto him. Perhaps it was because he was so weakened, but it worked; she felt it.

Hadeon laughed—a hollow, bitter sound. *You're a fool. The Great Ones don't care about us.* But his voice sounded less harsh and more worried as he spoke.

"They care about the balance," Inessa countered. "And

you're disrupting it. They will intervene, and their intervention will be catastrophic."

Hadeon's eyes flickered with uncertainty, a crack in his defiance. *I am what I am, and that is Death.*

"While that is true," Inessa said softly. "We can work together. You know you don't have to reap as often as you have been."

Hadeon's muzzle rested on the ground, and he turned to look at Hlíf who was weakened too. *I will try. If only to spare myself some grief from some surly gods.*

Inessa arched a brow and bit her tongue. There would be no apology, no making amends, only this weak response. She rubbed the bridge of her nose and grumbled. "That'll have to do. But for now, you'll allow life to fight back, and only when it has proven to be too much will we reap."

A flicker of torchlight brought Inessa's attention toward Hlíf. There, beside her stood a figure Inessa knew well—her father—his eyes were trained on the great wolf, and even from where she sat, she could see worry etched in his face.

Inessa's breath caught in her throat. Of course he'd stubbornly followed her when she told him not to. A small smile curved her lips as she stood.

Her father's eyes widened in awe. "By the gods..." he whispered, his voice filled with reverence. "Hlíf..."

Inessa hurried over, her heart pounding. "Father! You're here!"

His head jerked toward Inessa and relief flooded his face as he wrapped an arm around her. "You're alive!" He blinked, then looked down at Hlíf. "And she..." He withdrew from Inessa and reached out his hand, hesitating just before touching the majestic creature.

Hlíf lifted her head slightly, acknowledging him with a

weary but regal gaze. Her father knelt beside Hlíf, his rough hands gentle as he examined her for any wounds.

"She's all right." Inessa reassured. "She touched Hadeon."

Her father's brow rose in question. "They cannot touch each other?"

She shook her head. "No, it drains them."

"And is he..."

"Dead? You can't kill Death," Inessa said with a humorless laugh. "He is...considering things in a new light, I think."

His brows furrowed, and he walked toward where Stellan sat and Hadeon rested. The torchlight illuminated the shadowy figure of Hadeon and set Stellan in a warm glow. Why was it light always embraced him when it only highlighted her sharpness and shadows?

Her father knelt beside the fallen horse, inspecting him with a critical eye. "Can he truly be trusted?" he asked quietly. "He has taken so much."

"I don't trust him," Inessa said as she walked up behind him. "Not at all, but what I do trust is his desire to protect himself and his interests. If he wants to be remembered, if he wants to continue doing as he does—he will correct his path." She twisted her lips. "But I think he should be punished for what he has done. For every soul he has reaped during his gluttony, he should be imprisoned and bound for ten years."

Her father looked at her, his eyes searching her face. "How many souls has he taken?"

"Seven in the span of a fortnight."

"How will you bind him?"

Inessa wasn't certain. She looked to Hlíf. "I know you

can't without a great loss to yourself, but are we able to bind him to the Great Lodge with Stellan?"

Hlíf nodded. "I will grant the ability to keep him bound and he won't be able to reap. But there still must be Death, or we are back to the same problem. So, Inessa, you must continue your calling even as he's bound."

Her father made a noise in the back of his throat and said softly, "Your mother would be proud of you, Inessa."

Inessa swallowed roughly and motioned toward Stellan. "I couldn't have done it without Stellan."

At this, Stellan stood and extended his hand to her father. Her father clasped his forearm and brought him in for an embrace. "Thank you for protecting her."

"Oh," Stellan said, shooting Inessa a look. "She can handle herself, as I've seen. You've done a fine job, and your wife would be proud of the daughter *you* raised."

Despite not wanting them, tears sprung in her eyes and she shook her head. Maybe it was exhaustion and stress, or maybe the emotions came from thinking of how her mother would have viewed her. Would she actually have been proud?

"Great Ones, I'm standing right here." Now, they had to bind him for his punishment.

"Inessa, come take some of my fur," Hlíf said.

She did as she was prompted and gathered the fur.

"Now roll it into rope."

Inessa arched a brow. Rolling fur into rope wasn't exactly possible, but she did as she was asked. As she worked the fur in her fingers, it lengthened. When she needed more, she grabbed more fur to work with and soon she had a strand longer than she could measure. And it glowed just like Hlíf's beautiful pelt.

"Now, fashion a bridle with it, and he will be forced to walk with you."

Inessa walked over to Hadeon, and he didn't so much as look at her. His head remained on the ground, and she slid the makeshift bridle on him. The tether was still longer than she imagined.

Hadeon groaned deeply, almost as if he were whimpering.

"We must walk now," Hlíf said.

Everyone, including her father, walked to the Great Lodge.

Stellan pushed the doors open and Hlíf slowly entered, limping as she led the way to the altar.

Inessa held the lead as she fell behind with Hadeon who was struggling to walk. By the time she entered, the candles were lit and everyone awaited her.

Eventually, she made her way to the altar, and her eyes caught on the shadow at the corner. Hadeon.

"Inessa, lead him to the platform and properly bind him with the extra rope."

Inessa did just that, winding the cord around his legs, around his body and with every inch that touched him he grew weaker and weaker until his body rolled over, as bound as it was, and he wheezed.

"Stellan, draw blood from me," Hlíf ordered and nodded when her vessel hesitated.

Stellan approached her and drew out his knife, then carefully cut her paw. Instead of red blood, out poured the purest of gold liquid.

"Take it and rub it over the bindings as I speak." Hlíf limped forward, holding her head high as she looked to the rafters. Then, as she spoke, her gentle voice grew stronger, and filled the Great Lodge.

"By my power and the will of life,
I temper your name and end your strife.
Your deeds of ill now cease and bind,
No harm to others in body or mind.
For seventy cycles, let time hold fast,
A cage of justice until harm is past.
Bound by earth, by air, by sea, by fire,
Your harmful intent shall soon expire.
By law of balance, by rule of three,
As I will it, so mote it be."

And then, as Inessa stood from rubbing the last of the wolf's blood on the rope, Hadeon's body disappeared. No tether was left behind. Inessa whirled around, confused. "Where is he?"

"He is bound to the inbetween. Neither the heavens nor the earth. And he cannot return until his debt is paid."

Now Hlíf looked even weaker, her eyes more hollow. "I must go and rest, but as for everyone here, rebuild."

And live.

Fifteen

With the adrenaline no longer pumping through her veins, the trek home was a draining one. Inessa longed for her bed, yet her thoughts raced. Stellan had chosen to follow her home and had spent the journey talking to her father.

The notion brought butterflies to her stomach. It would be foolish to call what she felt for him love, but a liking? What wasn't to like about him? He was gentle, kind, and fierce.

When they finally came upon their home, her father led them inside. Inessa set to lighting the lamps and motioned for Stellan to take a seat, but he didn't. Instead, he knelt in front of the hearth and started a fire.

"Stellan, stay until the morning. You've had a long night so far. I have some bread from earlier, and some mead." Inessa's father grabbed a whole loaf from the cupboard and a pitcher of mead, then set about waiting on Stellan.

"I can do that," she said. Her gaze flicked to Stellan who smiled at her. With that simple gesture, she could nearly feel his arms around her, embracing her. Inessa cleared her throat and grabbed the goblets from the cupboard, then set them down in front of each chair. "Let me see that." She grabbed the loaf and pitcher and poured them each a cup, then set the loaf on the table and cut off large chunks for them too.

"Now, tell me, where do we go from here?" Her father asked.

"From here? I encourage life to fight off the plague that lingers still, and only if the souls are too weak, should there ever be a reaping." Stellan drank from his cup.

And Inessa would stave off the threat of a reaping, if she could help it. Unless it was required. If Hadeon started to forget the threat of the Great Ones, she'd remind him. She controlled him now, at least for the next seventy years.

RAYS OF SUNLIGHT TRICKLED THROUGH THE TREES, painting the earth in hues of pink and gold. Inessa sat before the lake, digging her fingers into the dirt to loosen the flat stones. The air was cool and refreshing, carrying the scent of ozone and freshly fallen pine limbs.

Despite not getting a decent night's rest, she felt lighter than she had in years. Perhaps that was what hope did, that and the promise of change, that life would blossom once more.

Footsteps snagged her attention from the glimmering lake and toward the approaching individual. Stellan peered down at her with a warm smile. "Inessa," he greeted, his voice filled with a tenderness that made her heart flutter.

She turned back to the lake and launched a rock,

watching as it skipped—once, twice, thrice—across the smooth surface.

After a moment, he settled down next to her, watching as she skipped rocks. "Inessa," Stellan spoke softly, his voice filled with emotion.

She looked at him, her eyes searching his. "What is it, Stellan?"

He took a deep breath, his gaze never leaving hers. "I need to head home. See to everyone else. Svetl is in a good place right now, but Runestadt..." He sighed, leaning into her. "The plague hit it hard. I need to check on my sister."

Inessa's heart constricted. He'd done so much for Svetl, more than she ever could thank him for. And his sister...gods. All she could see was the deathly pale girl sleeping on the pallet.

"There is another thing..." A strange, uncertain look passed over his features and he twisted his lips. "What if I said I want to see what the future holds for us? To see if it's you who will stand by my side until the Great Stallion comes to usher us to the Great Hall?"

Her brows lifted in surprise. She mulled over his words, carefully pulling them apart. He wasn't proposing marriage, only saying he wanted to see if she was the one for him, and yet her heart was racing so damn fast.

"A-are you sure you want to get to know me better? Some say I'm a völva you know, and that I'm touched by Death." She shot him a look, and he closed the distance between them. He pressed his lips to hers, reminding her of their time shared in his home.

Every nerve ending came to life. *Life.*

He inspired life inside of her. But what did she give him?

"Tell me this, what do I give you?" she whispered against his lips. "You are warm, gentle and kind and I'm—"

"Strong, resilient, and warmer than you realize. You have held yourself apart from your people, so afraid to touch them with D eath." Stellan none too gently pulled her into his lap so that she straddled him. "You cannot touch me with Death, Inessa." He brushed his nose against her ear. "We are two halves to a whole, and to answer your question—you are what I am not, in the best ways."

Inessa cupped his face and leaned her forehead against his. Closing her eyes, she let his words sink in. She was enough for him.

"In this moment, I give you—us—a chance to live."

His pale brows rose, and he grinned. "Who says a death-bringer can't bring life?" Stellan winked and said no more as Inessa silenced him with her lips.

Her journey had been long and arduous, but it had brought them to this moment—a moment of hope, and a promise for the future. And though Stellan would return home shortly, Inessa knew he'd return, and maybe together, they could conquer anything.

Preview the next book in
A HORDE OF DEAD POETS
collection!

AVAILABLE NOW

One

The middle of our one-room precinct, sitting across from my partner Raphael Sinclair at our shared desk, was the wrong place to be obsessed with learning about my lineage. There was no privacy in this small space. Only the chief had the illusion of such with her glass-enclosed office on the opposite side of our open-floor breakroom.

At any moment one of the other three detectives could find my feverish study of the journal I held in my hand more interesting than the case they were supposed to be reviewing.

But I didn't care. I was too caught up in a snare of discovery and sense of betrayal.

A spasm of pain shot down my legs. The knot just above my tailbone throbbed. Dryness clawed at the back of my throat. But I ignored all of it. And just kept reading.

> We are lost in the midst of imbalance. I shall find the point of intersection.
> BALANCE

~~I will kill all the good and save all the evil and still it won't work.~~
NO NO NO NO. GOOD MUST WIN. NOT EVIL.

THERE IS NO BALANCE

"There is no balance," I whispered, trying out the words written in the journal and searching my mind for the meaning missing from the page. Had she given up trying to find the balance? Or had she concluded there wasn't a way to keep it?

"What?" my partner, Raphael, asked.

"Nothing," I said and finally picked up my coffee and took a drink. The creak of the rotating ceiling fan needled at my nerves. They still hadn't repaired our air-conditioning. Nervous energy sent electric pinpricks along my bare arms, making me flush.

Last weekend, I'd started to clean the attic in my childhood home. It wasn't the first time since my mother's passing five years ago that cleaning out the house became my priority. And each time I tried, I always ended up with piles of stuff I could never give away. Too much history in those walls. Both good and bad. The bad memories kept me from ever living there. A promise to my dying mother kept me from selling it.

All the women on my mother's side of the family had kept journals. Some filled with love and adventure and others filled with their own variations of the practices and rituals passed down from my 5th great grandma, Felicia LaRue, who lived in the house in the late 1800s. Most of her earlier journals were dedicated to her craft. Over the years, her entries had grown darker and more fatalistic in nature. Like something or someone had corrupted her soul. But it never spoke of specifics regarding what had caused this shift in her being.

I'd made a home for the journals I could display on a bookshelf, handcrafted by a local carpenter, and had arranged them by date. My one contribution to the home, aside from the yearly maintenance and overall upkeep of the place. It made me feel more like a caretaker than a previous occupant of the house.

And now, I had to find a place for the diaries I'd recently found buried in a box of sewing material, bound together with red velvet fabric. Because these could not go on display. While the dark content reminded me of Grandma Felicia's journals, these ramblings were much more and everything to do with the torment and cruelty of being a Champion for Good and Evil.

During Mardi Gras earlier this year, I'd met the human embodiment of evil. He called himself Papa Sin. And after helping me solve a case in which he was directly involved, he told me I was a Champion for Good and Evil. And six months later, I still had no idea what that enormous title entailed.

I kneaded the small of my back with my fist, trying to work out a knot. I'd been hunched over for what seemed like hours now, furiously reading each page with a single-minded determination to find answers to my dilemma.

The first in this series of journals written by my grandma Lucille had already shown signs of her mind breaking. Incoherent thoughts intermingled with details of people she encountered. Individuals she had judged to be either good or evil and the small influences she'd had on their lives. She sounded like a master manipulator—whispering in a person's ear—swaying them one way or the other. All to restore balance. At least that's what she had written about herself.

I convinced him to kill his friend. It was the only way to restore balance.

My memories of my grandmother had always been filled with joy and happiness. She'd come to live with us after my father's death. The abuse my mother and I had endured for years had been kept from her, and she spent her last days helping us heal. Now, those memories were tainted with the knowledge of all the twisted things she had done.

Would I become like her?

There had to be more journals, ones she began when she first met Papa Sin and Mama Root. Right? I kept going back to that thought. Yet every search since had yielded no results. The frustration of it was wearing on me.

"Learn anything?" Raphael asked abruptly.

"Well," I said with a sigh, looking across the desk at him. "I might end up going crazy."

Raphael tilted his head to the side. "We won't let that happen."

I gave him a quick smile and looked away. I wish he could stop my eventual descent into madness. Because despite only seeing two instances of my ancestor's struggle with mental health, I knew they all had. I just hadn't found all the proof yet.

The precinct phone rang, pulling everyone's attention. "Silverwood Police Department. How may I direct your call?" Our receptionist looked at us, then after a beat, frowned and shook her head. "No, Mrs. Clark, they haven't moved the grocery store. Is Billy around?"

The Silverwood, Georgia police department had five

detectives and twenty patrol officers for the twenty-seven thousand residents, most of whom were well into the senior years. We had our share of crime but most of it occurred during and after the tourist season.

On days like this, Chief Declouette had us going through what she'd dubbed as the 'Fresh Eyes' review. Old cases were brought out and exchanged between the five detectives to see if we could find any new leads. No one liked that sort of scrutiny of their work.

My partner Raphael and I were looking through an old hit and run. My quick read-through let me know we were never going to solve it. The driver wasn't a local. The plates were stolen. And every drunken eyewitness statement read like a fever-dream, with varying degrees of lunacy intertwined. Rarely did we find witnesses who astutely observed what was going on around them. Which meant most statements were filled with fabrications and embellishments with only a kernel of truth thrown in. And it was our job to weed through all of it.

With a heavy sigh, I returned to my own search. And tried not to think about how it was also turning out to be pointless.

The next few pages were more of the same. It was as if Grandma Lucille's mind was slowly deteriorating. Like she was screaming in her head and nobody was listening. One entry was dated the year before she died. All I remember from that time was the joy she had in my college acceptance. I pictured her on the day I left. Mouth stretched wide in a smile, while tears of joy streamed down her face. *"You have somethin' in you that will make you a great officer, my little Beatrice. Somethin' great."*

Now her words held a deeper meaning. She had known

what I was and would become one day. Police. Why didn't she warn me? Why didn't she tell me about all the horrific things she had done and the ways in which I might be forced to do the same?

But I wished she'd told us she was suffering.

I turned the page.

This was the end of everything. I read the date. A few weeks before she died, she had covered the page with a single message:

We are born in sin. We are born in sin. We are born in sin.

And the last line:

Just twisted souls upon the Tree of Life.

None of her previous journals had references to Christianity or any other religion, so why was she talking about sin?

I got up and went to the breakroom, needing a minute to think. The coffee was gone, and my throat was still dry. After retrieving a bottle of water from the refrigerator, I cracked the sealed cap, leaned against the counter and sipped—thoughts on that single line.

Just twisted souls upon the Tree of Life.

The first idea that came to mind was puppetry. Our souls like marionettes hung from branches, jerking and dancing until their strings tangled. Was that what Champions were? And what would that make the Tree of Life? The puppeteer, a great manipulator.

I rubbed the knot on my back again, wondering if there would be any point in requesting an ergonomic chair. I needed to move. Do something. All this sitting around couldn't be good for me.

"Well, damn," one of the detectives yelled out. "It's been three months since his execution and seems one of them streaming services is doing a documentary on the Pasadena Butcher."

Everyone groaned. I hated those shows. Always romanticizing and embellishing on the life of some deranged killer for ratings. Completely forgetting about the pain their victims' families endured. In this case, the Butcher had killed over sixty women before he was caught, not by a confession but a selfie one of his victims had sent before her death.

I returned to my desk and sat down heavily in my uncomfortable chair. I might have to buy my own. Raphael spared me a brief glance, then resumed his reading, a smile stretching across his face.

I looked down at the journal again.

We are born in sin. We are born in sin. We are born in sin. Just twisted souls upon the Tree of Life.

"Damnit!" I yelled.

Raphael looked up. "You all right over there?"

I stared at him, shaking my head. "I'm missing something. I know I am."

He just stared at me, his warm brown eyes assessing. "Take a break." A smile slowly stretched across his face. "Look at it with...fresh eyes."

"You are not funny," I said, laughing. "I'm almost done."

"Good. Then we can go grab some lunch at Lewis' Catfish and Po Boys."

"Sounds like a plan."

I flipped through the last few pages, all covered in the same message. My hopes of learning anything more died with each page turned. Something had driven my grandmother to this point of hopelessness. To the point that she stopped trying to find balance and focused all her energy on sin.

I got to the last page of the journal and stopped.

A phantom pain slowly crawled down my spine.

Unable to breathe, I stared at the macabre drawing of The Tree of Life. Its vines were twisted and grotesque. Limbs withered with decay oozing out of the cracks. Done in a realistic style, the ink drawing seemed to pulse with life. I ran my finger along the page and could feel the rough indentations her pencil left on the cream-colored paper. Resting in the thick of brambles and dead leaves were tiny boxes filled with a single phrase.

We are but twisted souls on The Tree of Life.

Something about the tree mesmerized me, as if I were being pulled into the space where it existed on those cream-colored pages. I could almost feel a cool wind caressing my face. Smell the damp soil in which this twisted, majestic oak rested. The branches moved, swaying in the breeze. I lifted my hand and ran a finger along the ridge-covered leaf. Like a message in brail had been imprinted on them. I closed my eyes against the wind and concentrated on what I was feeling.

Just twisted souls upon the tree of life.

My heart pounded in my chest; the sound pulsed against my eardrums. A hallow ache formed in my throat. Raw and unyielding. I swallowed the emotion. The world tilted and filled with a dark pulsing sky. It reminded me of the first time I spotted the Sin Exchange. A way station that sat at the crossroads, connecting the entire world to a single pop-up shop where Mama Root tended her herbs.

"We are born in sin. We are born in sin. We are born in sin," A soft voice chanted in my head. My chest heaved and the image blurred. I was once again sitting rooted in my chair, eyes glued to the image. The ink on the page swirled, the branches forming words...no, names...I touched the page and felt warmth on my fingertips.

"Bee!"

I jerked, and slammed the journal shut—the sound suddenly cutting off. I shook my head and stared across the desk at my partner. His image wavered for a bit; I blinked a few times bringing him into focus.

Before I could show Raphael what I'd found, a commotion broke out at the front of the precinct. I turned and found a woman standing in the lobby with tears in her eyes.

"I'd like to talk to someone about my aunt's murder."

ENJOY THESE NOVELLAS IN ANY ORDER!

A HORDE OF DEAD POETS

Acknowledgments

Thank you for reading Death's Maiden! It was a tough year to write this, as I not only lost my grandmother but my husband lost his grandfather—six weeks apart.

I started this novella not knowing how difficult the year would turn out, but that is precisely why I infused a sense of hope within it too...where there is death there will be life.

I want to thank Carla and Jess for shaping this novella into what it is. Heaven knows it was a mess when I turned it in... so huge thanks, ladies.

This is my last piece I'll be publishing, as I have made the decision to retire from writing. So, I hope you enjoyed and will look into my backlist.

Much love,

Elle Beaumont

About Elle Beaumont

 Elle Beaumont loves creating vivid and fantastical worlds. She lives in South-eastern Massachusetts with her husband and two children. When not writing or chasing around her children, she enjoys making candles. More than once she has proclaimed that coffee is the lifeblood and it is how she refrains from becoming a zombie.

Stay up to date and receive some free books by signing up for her newsletter! ellebeaumontbooks.com/newsletter

Join Elle's Facebook group and hang out with her facebook.com/groups/ElleBeaumontStreetTeam

For more information visit
www.ellebeaumontbooks.com

More from Elle Beaumont

Standalones

The Castle of Thorns

The Dragon's Bride

Benvolio & Mercutio Turn Back Time

Beneath the Willow

Anthologies

Something in the Shadows

Link by Link

Beyond the Cogs

Emporium of Superstition

The Darkest Lullaby

Immortal Realms Trilogy

Seeds of Sorrow

Tides of Torment

Wages of War

The Hunter Series

Hunter's Truce

Royal's Vow

Assassin's Gambit

Queen's Edge

Secrets of Galathea

Brotherhood

Bindings

Voice

King

Demons of Frosteria

Slaying the Frost King

Frost Mate

Frost Claim